COMMON BOUNDARY

Stories of Immigration

COMMON BOUNDARY
Stories of Immigration

Edited By

GREGORY F. TAGUE

Editions Bibliotekos, Inc.

E◆B

Brooklyn, New York

Editions Bibliotekos
Great Books – Uncommon Readers

Fredericka A. Jacks, Publisher

Proofreader: Kristen Morale

EBibliotekos@gmail.com
www.ebibliotekos.blogspot.com

Printed & Bound in the United States

Set in Garamond

ISBN: 978-0982481936

Editions Bibliotekos, Inc.
E♦B
Brooklyn, New York

"All the world is one."

-   John Wesley

CONTENTS

Notes on Contributors, &
Publication Acknowledgments

PREFACE

Fredericka A. Jacks

Once, after we had picked up our daughter from kindergarten, we found a note in her bag from the school nurse saying that she had a "speech problem." The Principal insisted this was so, that there was a firm diagnosis, and that we should not delay in seeking professional help. Of course we knew this not to be true and emphasized to the Principal (again) that our daughter had come to the United States (nearly four years old) speaking only Lithuanian. For the most part, we spoke only English. Our daughter had moved from one monolingual environment to another.

Complications that arose because of the clash of languages seemed irresolvable. People continually asked, "How's her English?" We were also asked, routinely, if she spoke Russian or Polish – "Isn't Lithuanian similar?" After a few years, many of the same people then asked, "Do you think she remembers any of her *own* language?" A culture is a country's language, its customs, and the collective thinking or attitude of the people; our daughter was a little immigrant who had brought with her an entire culture. Not surprisingly, there was no speech problem; rather, there was ignorance on the part of others about the particular word inflections made by our daughter as she moved from one language to another.

Common Boundary includes many varieties of immigration stories. The shifting attitude we experienced over our daughter's English acquisition (and the loss of her native language) represents a paradox: on the one hand, there is an attempt to accommodate someone from another country; on the other hand, the immigrant person is always perceived as something foreign. There's a common boundary – being *part of* and yet being *apart from* others.

Our editorial approach, considering that this is a collection of creative writings, has been light-handed: we permit each writer to speak in his or her own voice, with its own distinctive rhythm, syntax, and idiom. We are delighted to present this multi-vocal volume and trust that not only will you find each contribution compelling to read but also will discover how the book (later) is worth pondering in its cumulative, overall emotional and intellectual effect.

FOREWORD

Jason Dubow

In a post-9/11 world increasingly shrunk by the power of technology and the possibility of mobility, immigration is as much in the news as it has ever been. The details of that news – this bill, that crackdown, a bar graph here, some commentary there – are flat and fleeting. The lasting news, the news that gives depth to our understanding of the world and humanity, is elsewhere – in stories, in *these* stories: *these* people, *these* places, *these* things. The news is in a young girl's memory of the "slivers of what had once been her father's violin" as she flees Nazi-infected Hungary ("They Set Sail in Springtime"); the news is the struggle of a Mexican immigrant to make sense (for herself and others) of a giant Peruvian potato displayed at a Midwestern state fair ("La Santa Papa"); and the news is in the worried father preparing to bring his newly-adopted daughter "home" from China "towards [what he believes is] a future of hope and promise" in Brooklyn ("The Plain Brown Envelopes"). The news is in the spices, the photographs, and the furniture; the news is in individual struggles, memories, and hopes.

My grandmother, Nana Ruth, would have loved *Common Boundary: Stories of Immigration* (or, as I persistently misread the last word of the title, "*Imagination*") because, as an immigrant herself (a Holocaust refugee), she would have found *naches* ("joy") in both the familiar ("Wooden Trunk from Buchenwald") and the unfamiliar. These stories of immigration (*and* imagination) are about people, like my grandmother, who mentally and emotionally live between places, languages, and cultures. And, really, aren't we all a jumble of perspectives? Aren't we all living somewhere between our dreams and our reality, between our fears and our desires, between our various identities? Maybe President Franklin D. Roosevelt was right, at least metaphorically, when he famously said, "We are all immigrants." Haven't we all, to take liberties with song writers Simon and Garfunkel, gone to look for *our* "America"?

If "[being] a foreigner means speaking without being understood" ("Blue Painted Field"), then the writers here are anything but: they speak and you will understand. You'll like some pieces better than others (who knows, or cares, why). I have my favorites – "Living Between Question Marks," "An Immigrant's Deal" – but I can easily imagine why any one of these pieces might be *your* favorite. As it's true that we are "nothing if not an anthology of our experiences and the places we've lived" ("Beginning in the Midwest"), then this book is really an anthology of anthologies: a collection of stories in which the old inextricably blends with the new, in which the tensions between what has been lost and what can be gained are grappled with (but, inevitably, not resolved), and in which the human capacity to imagine a future and make it real (more or less) is explored from a variety of different perspectives. Here's the essential question: now that I am no longer *there* but *here*, Who am I? The answers, the *stories* – various, contingent, authentic – have made me, in a Whitman-esque sense, "larger," and they will you too. And so, when you're done reading, ask yourself: Who *now* am I?

How He Made It Across

Patty Somlo

The tenth time the agent asked Alejandro how he made it across, Alejandro gave him the same short weary answer.

"Sir, I walked."

Alejandro was not too tall, with already-dark skin browned further by the sun. His straight black hair looked as if it had been cut with the use of a bowl. He did not raise his head when he spoke.

The agent stood next to Alejandro's chair, his right calf brushing the metal leg. He marched over to the desk and back, his steps heavy due to his substantial weight. If Alejandro had stood up, the agent would have towered over him by at least a foot. The agent's hair was cut military style, and a pair of sunglasses hung like a weapon from his front uniform pocket.

Alejandro breathed in the acrid aroma of old coffee spilling from the agent's breath. The agent had just leaned down, his face a few inches from Alejandro's forehead.

"How did you make it across?" The agent paused, momentarily, after assaulting Alejandro with each word in slow motion for the eleventh time.

Alejandro hadn't eaten for over twenty-four hours. His head ached and his stomach had grown sour. His mother had taught him always to tell the truth, but the truth didn't appear to be what the agent wanted.

"I walked across, sir," Alejandro repeated for the eleventh time.

If the agent had known the entire truth, he would have needed to step outside, spit violently into the street, then stomp to the corner, yank open the heavy wooden door leading into Jake's Bar, barely allowing his eyes to adjust, before blindly making his way over to the bar and demanding a double Jack Daniel's on the rocks. What the agent didn't know was that Alejandro Murghia Lopez left his village in the south of Mexico, close to the Guatemalan border, on a Monday, before the sun had come up. Teptapa was a mere sigh in the dusty road from Mexico City to Tegucigalpa, a town barely suggested by a tired *tienda* with an oft broken-down generator that kept lemon-lime and sweet orange *refrescos* cold. Yet, on a morning that was still cool and dark, Alejandro felt as if he were leaving more than a shrug of earth behind. He understood that he was also abandoning his life.

The distance was unfathomable. Being a simple man who believed in God, the Virgin Mary and the spirits of the corn, rain, moon and sun, Alejandro hadn't bothered to discover how far America was from Teptapa. Funny thing, Alejandro didn't know what America looked like, so how would he know once he arrived? He carried a few cold tortillas, a cupful of beans and another of rice, and a jar filled with water. On his feet, he wore a pair of Nike knockoffs a distant cousin had brought back from Tijuana.

By the fourth day of walking, Alejandro had lost track of time. He walked in the daylight and continued to walk at night. When he couldn't walk anymore, he lay down to rest in doorways and under bridges and once even in an abandoned car.

The agent's head hurt, from his temples to a spot in back above his neck. *This job is getting to me.* That's what he said to his girl, Maria, at the bar last night, every time she begged him to dance. He'd planned to stick to Coors, since he needed to get up for work at five. But all the damned beer did was fill him up. That's why he started in on dark, sweet, 100-proof rum.

They'd finished the new fence and couldn't understand how these cockroaches were still getting across. Computers, cameras, night-vision equipment and stuff the agent was still learning to operate were designed to alert the agents if anyone tried to cut a hole. The cameras were set to take a photograph and trip an alarm the second an illegal tried to get across.

So, how did the fucker do it? The agent sure wanted to know. His head was pounding something awful. He'd already taken enough painkillers to put a man out.

"You walked?" the agent said, his right hand clutching the back of the chair where the little Mexican sat. He looked like an Indian to the agent.

"Yes, sir," Alejandro whispered.

"What'd you say?"

"I walked, sir," Alejandro replied, more loudly now.

Alejandro had grown dizzy as the last day wore on. Luckily, he was still headed in the right direction. The poor man wouldn't have known if he'd gotten turned around. He had dreamed of coming to America for even longer than he could remember. His desire to reach the place had become the engine moving him forward, as the power in his legs was wearing out.

"What I'm trying to figure out is how'd you get past the fence?" The agent had pulled a wooden toothpick from his pocket and began to use it to clean the spaces between his top front teeth.

"I don't understand," Alejandro said, ashamed that his English was so poor.

"*La frontera*," the agent shouted, the Spanish words carrying the twang of South Texas. *"Como te vas atras?"*

The agent mumbled under his breath, without waiting for Alejandro's response. *How the fuck did you do it?*

Alejandro shuffled his feet and tried to calm the beating of his heart. He saw himself sitting on his porch back in Teptapa. What he couldn't explain was how a man feels, right before the sun comes up, when the silence of the long black night suddenly gets broken by the rooster's morning call. Alejandro couldn't have described the way his spirit grew large and lifted him up, watching the fiery orange ball stretch up into the sky, streaked with shredded pink clouds. He had a good idea the agent wouldn't understand that as the sun climbed, lighting up the fields, Alejandro began to believe he could do anything he wanted.

"Did you pay a *coyote?* Did someone help you across?" the agent asked now.

Alejandro slowly shook his head from side to side. He couldn't explain that the man sitting in this chair was not the one who left Teptapa over a month before. That man, he was ashamed to admit, had collapsed onto the ground before he even had a chance to try and make it across. At the moment when he hit the dirt, he was on the Mexican side, so close to America it would have taken only a few steps north to get across. His body dropped and the dust rose all around. For some reason, the wind suddenly picked up.

The wind is to blame, Alejandro wanted to say. Instead, he swallowed the words, just as they began to form in his mouth.

The agent walked heavily across the linoleum floor and out the door. Moving from the chilled air inside, the agent felt as if he'd been slapped with a hot dry towel. He looked down the road, where the air wavered above the pavement. A cold beer would taste awfully good right now, he thought.

Dust buried the tips of his boots a few minutes after he started to walk. He knew it was against patrol procedures to leave an alien alone in the office un-cuffed. If the truth be told, the agent hoped Alejandro would take off. He understood that the Mexican wasn't about to tell him how he made it across. He'd let the little guy vanish, and both of them would be off the hook.

By the time the agent returned to the office, after nursing one cold Coors Light, Alejandro was heading toward San Diego. He had gone past the point of hunger. He understood that on the Mexican side of the border something otherworldly had taken place – the man he had been was turned into dust after his last breath released itself and his heart made one final clap. The dust of Alejandro Murghia Lopez, a poor farmer from Teptapa, lifted into the wind above the border and drifted across. As it cleared the fence, meant to keep Mexicans like Alejandro out, the dust didn't even bother to hide.

Alejandro entered the city of San Diego at dusk. It took him no time to blend in with the other men from villages where light at night came from the stars.

Months after, he found himself on a warm clear evening, looking up at the sky. He imagined that the poor farmer from Teptapa was hanging suspended there, wondering whether coming to America had been worth giving up his life. At that moment, the quiet, copper-skinned man assured his old self that he was glad he had made it to the other side. Though life wasn't easy, as the poor farmer had so often fantasized, this American guy, Al Lopez, was doing all right.

◊ ～◆～ ◊

"And now I'm in the world alone,
Upon the wide, wide sea . . ."

-     Lord Byron

"The whole world is a person's birthplace."

-     Statius

◊ ～◆～ ◊

Monologue from *Migrations*

Cassandra Lewis

In *Migrations* two families living next door to each other in San Francisco's Mission District explore the connection between blood origins and lives created by individual aspirations. After a young mother, Solana Rivera, refuses to pay "garbage fees" to her landlord she is arrested for living in the U.S. without a green card and faced with the decision of leaving her American-born baby behind with her neighbors or bringing him with her to prison.

PEDRO RIVERA: male, Mexican-American, 38.

PEDRO

We were kept in prison here for two months before we were sent back to Mexico. Then we failed the first time we tried to cross. A friend of our family's introduced us to a new coyote. The man who helped us years before had been killed by a group of men with guns in Texas – not government workers – a vigilante militia. So our family found new help for us.

This new coyote was known for his night trails. We traveled with only the moonlight to guide us. The desert isn't all sand like in the movies. Much of it is covered by tall weeds that dry out and tear your skin. The coyote carried a machete and hacked the weeds that hid us from the helicopters. I can still hear the swoosh of his blade. After a while you get a rhythm going. Swoosh, step. Swoosh, step.

When we got to Nogales, Arizona, we hid behind a gas station while the coyote went to use the pay phone. He said he was calling his wife, but really he called the border patrol. They paid him a finder's fee. We were arrested and sent back.

The second time we tried to cross we paid another coyote to help us. That coyote guided us way off the agreed upon route and met up with a truck driver. We hadn't agreed to any truck ride, but by then we had spent all of our family's money and felt it was too late to turn back. We had just about made it to the border. This truck could get us across.

Solana and I secretly agreed that as soon as we crossed the border we would leave the truck and the coyote before anything else could happen. The sides of the truck had paintings of orange bottles with cartoon faces. Normally it carried sodas and was supposed to have refrigeration. But when the driver opened the back we saw no sodas. Instead there were dozens of terrified faces. We squeezed past the others until we got to the back. He slammed the door and locked it.

Complete darkness. The air felt thick and used. The summer heat from outside and the heat from all of our bodies crammed together, packed so tightly we couldn't even sit down, thickened with each breath. We were slowly suffocating. We had no water. I don't know how many days we were stuck in there. But when the driver finally opened the door the daylight was like lasers on my skin, piercing my eyes so that in the newfound light I still could not see. When he finally opened the door Solana was not breathing. Half of us were dead.

◊ ~◆~ ◊

"Strange the world about me lies
Never yet familiar grown –
Still disturbs me with surprise,
Haunts me like a face half known."

- William Watson

"Custom reconciles us to everything."

- Edmund Burke

◊ ~◆~ ◊

The Unmasking of El Santo

George Rabasa

Benito Segura feels the weight of tradition. Before Gorgeous George or Jesse Ventura or The Rock or Stone Cold Steve Austin, there was El Santo. Benito owns the look: silver Speedo trunks over pearly gray tights; high-tops bright with metallic polish. He unfurls the satin cape in the mirror, his brown hairless chest glistening with baby oil, snaking muscles along the arms and shoulders, belly sucked into the waistband. El Santo keeps himself buff. The shiny satin mask – with the slits for eyes, like a wildcat's, and the outline of the mouth, thick lips curling with contempt – remains un-violated. Even in this incarnation, nobody can put a lock on El Santo. The identity of the unknown paladin is still secret.

Benito waits for adventure. He knows the bad elements of the neighborhood, the boys in the gangas and the dealers in the alley. He came to St. Paul from Uruapan twenty years ago, an experienced pastry baker with the memorized recipes of a hundred pandulces: conchas, corbatas, chilindrinas, cuernitos, chalupas, orejas, huesitos, cocoles, vidrios, polvorones . . . Now, he sits behind Panadería La Esperanza, taking a break from the rolling of dough for bolillos and teleras. A bandana keeps the flour out of his hair, but his arms are streaked with masa and his fingertips stained brown from the hot sugar. He drinks sweet coffee in the alley and hangs with the vagos, listens to their bragging, their mocking jokes, their nudging snickers when a girl walks by. He remembers their boasts. Nobody knows that at night Benito goes out as El Santo and looks for the opportunity to mess things up for the bad guys.

On this Saturday night, El Santo cruises Robert and Concord Streets, then across the river to Bloomington and Lake, riding low in a '59 Impala, stealthy around the corners like a mountain lion. Wherever trouble happens, El Santo will be there, ready to defend the weak and the old, the soft and naive, children and grandmothers, and women in tight dresses.

Action at last: Two guys in a Ford Explorer, gringuitos with yellow hair, out to score some crank. El Santo parks in the shadows and rushes out from behind a building waving his cape. The dopers scream, holy shit! and get back in their car to peel out, thinking they have seen a ghost. Meanwhile, the two dealers chase El Santo until he loses them in a lightning sprint into the dark. The cabrones curse him and yell, chinga tu madre, and say if we ever find out who you are, pendejo, you will be hurting bad. Benito's heart goes haywire;

he whispers a panicked appeal to the Virgen de Guadalaupe. Mother of God!

The following Monday, word of the crime busting gets around. The customers in the bakery are buzzing about El Santo, a real hero of the community. But they add sadly, whoever he is, once he is found out, he is road-kill. Benito, naked to the waist, appears from behind the ovens, wiping the sweat off his face with the edge of his long apron. He says he knows who El Santo is. Nobody believes him. Just wait and see, Benito grins. He is dying to tell.

La Santa Papa

In the Summer of her sophomore year, Leticia Suarez finally scored a real job. She had looked for weeks, from coffee places to juice places to burrito places. The only things she got were occasional babysitting evenings for some of her parents' friends. She was a gifted babysitter; kids loved her and parents trusted her. So, it was no surprise when, after applying for a ten day gig at the Minnesota State Fair, she ended up babysitting a giant potato.

"Whatever," she said in that calculated insouciance she had perfected, the subtle shrug and eye roll adopted from the anglo girls in her school. Ni modo, she thought.

Alone inside the dusky tent, Leti is still, her sneakered feet planted on the hard ground, her slender frame swimming in green overalls with *Taterville Farm* stenciled on the bib. She works the second shift at the State Fair, from 4:00 until the lights are turned off, the thump of bass fades from the grandstand, and the crowds shuffle off. All this happens around midnight. She shuts her eyes tight and digs into her mind for the voice she thinks she hears inside her head.

Eight hours is forever, missing out on the last of summer, hearing the screams from the midway rides, smelling mini donuts and cheese curds frying all around. Occasionally, yearning for sunlight, Leti steps outside the tent; self-consciousness grips her when she realizes she is the only Mexican in a sea of pink faces. And then, there are rules: no cell phone, no ear buds, no socializing. Yet, since the third day these haven't been sacrifices. Leti feels a calling to be here.

She perks up when kids her age wander into the exhibit. She is friendly to them, but, as a Minneapolis girl, knows herself to be superior to the 4H types from outstate. They are such wide eyed bumpkins. She likes how they go quiet as soon as she cues the ethereal new age music, turns on the spotlight, and they face the massive contours of the "World's Biggest Potato."

Hyperspud rests on a pedestal, exuding a velvety radiance under a cone of light that beams down the center pole. The giant potato is set off behind a picket fence so that visitors won't reach out to touch its velvety surface, their fingers rubbing lesions onto the skin.

As people wander in, usually tentative, wary of being scammed by a sideshow, Leti collects tickets, adjusts the volume in her microphone, and announces, "Hyperspud welcomes you." That gets an occasional giggle because her pronunciation of the giant potato comes out as "jaipersput" no matter how hard she tries to get the soft *h* and the ambiguous *u* to sound right.

Once everyone has quieted down, she starts with a quick history of potatoes. She tells how they originated in Peru, South America, and were brought to Europe by the Spanish conquistadors, their popularity spreading to Germany, France, and, notably, Ireland. Then, full circle back to North America. This particular potato was harvested in the Taterville Farm in Eden, near Twin Falls, Idaho. It weighs about eighty pounds, is 4'11" tall and comes to her chin when she stands next to it. It's 32" around at its widest. It has a thousand eyes. (She made this up, but she likes the idea of all those eyes gazing out from the very depths of the giant.)

The floor of the tent is packed earth; when more than four people come inside, they kick up a fine dust which Leticia can taste and smell no matter that she shuts her mouth and holds her breath. When visitors are few, the dust settles, and she can smell the potato's mealy, starchy scent just like a potato bin in any cellar. Gawkers ask if the potato is real; she answers, "Oh yes," with assurance. "This thing is totally real."

She's encouraged to answer most questions even though she's been supplied only sketchy information. "You'll sound like an expert soon enough," she was told when she got the job. "Just see that everyone hears the same story." By the second day she had memorized the basics. Name: Hyperspud. Baking time: 36 hours at 450°, assuming you had a large enough oven. Species: Tuberous Idahoensis. Fertilizers: 100% organic. Soil: #3 clay base, high potash. Nutritional Info: 35,000 calories, 276 grams protein, 3580 carbohydrates. The facts roll around in her mind even when the tent is empty.

There are times she knows she's not totally alone. The din of the fair seems far away, muffled by the heavy canvas, and it is just she and Hyperspud. There's nothing to do but daydream, and keep each other company.

On that memorable third day of the ten-day job, Leti was asked a question that stumped her. A boy had come in with his father. This visit to the World's Biggest Potato was clearly about Dad, who had the bland uncurious attitude of suburban types, trying to entertain his kid. The boy was around five. He looked out of large eyes that seemed perpetually surprised, as if at the moment of being born he hadn't been able to believe what he'd come into. Now, years later, he was still looking around in amazement.

"Ask the lady how many zillion French fries will come out of that thing," the dad said, poking at his kid.

The boy shrugged in embarrassment. He raised his eyes toward the potato, and asked tentatively, "What's going to happen to Hyperspud when the fair is over?"

Leti had been rattling off her scientific facts, but grew quiet as she searched for an answer. Nobody had asked her that. She wondered if people didn't care, or if they just assumed the giant potato would be chopped and fried into pieces. She was about to blurt that out when something held her back. Perhaps it was the innocent look on the boy's face, or the eyes of the potato which seemed to be gazing unwaveringly in her direction.

"Why, it will go back to Lima, Peru, the home of its ancestors," she said. "To retire at the peak of its career.

Hyperspud will rest on a pedestal, in a central room of the potato museum, El Museo de la Papa, and just enjoy the fame to old age. It has to be a dark place, because as you know potatoes have sensitive eyes. And giant potatoes such as Hyperspud even more so."

After the boy left and Leti had perched back on her stool, she heard a long sigh mingled with soft hums of satisfaction. She wondered if another visitor had slipped into the tent but saw no one. It was just she and the potato; nobody else would be able to confirm that in fact there had been a breath exhaled from deep within Hyperspud. She looked in its direction; in the cone of light, its hundreds of eyes appeared to narrow in quiet contentment. Slowly, words meant for her alone rang out in the empty tent.

On this, the last day of the Fair, la Santa Papa is speaking again. The voice is a deep contralto, resonant with a chesty power. Leticia has been praying for this, the expectation warming her heart even when she's lonely, restless, and envious of the kids outside. The voice makes it all worthwhile.

Hijita, La Santa Papa is pleased with Leti.

Islamorada

Rivka Keren

Translated from the Hebrew by Dalit Shmueli

During the twilight hours of one day in January, the professor and his wife arrived at a small motel on the beach at Islamorada and checked in. After the New Year's Eve parties, the place had emptied of guests. It was hot and humid. Seaweed and snails piled up along the main road. Alongside the boats that docked in the marina, pelicans stood like statues on beams of rotted wood.

The couple was exhausted and sweaty after their long drive. They showered, changed into clean clothes, and went downstairs. They passed by the vending machines and ice dispenser, walked past the pool and crossed the lawn. Plastic cups rolled around in the wind. The rear parking lot was desolated, and the woman stopped for a moment, as if hesitating. A narrow path led to the ocean. They walked slowly, hand in hand, careful not to trip in their sandals. The coastline curved in a series of wide bays. Beach chairs were scattered haphazardly, and the couple pulled together two of them, brushed them off, and sat down.

Finally, said the professor.

They sat silently. The sea, like a full sail in the wind, rippled before their eyes in changing colors from turquoise, to indigo, to purple, and soon became cloaked in a coppery hue.

It's beautiful here, said the woman. But deserted.

That's what we wanted, isn't it, said the professor. He reminded his wife why they had left Jerusalem.

Maybe . . . said his wife. In the waning daylight her eyes followed a large seagull that was pecking among the seashells. The shadow of a lone boat loomed on the horizon. Gradually the sky became strewn with diamonds, and the couple gazed at them as they each sank into their own thoughts. The cry of a saxophone came from somewhere in the distance. High tide made little bites into the shoreline, leaving a white lace edging, rhythmically lapping like the sound of a nursing baby.

Now all was quiet. The music had been silenced and nothing could be heard but the gentle ebb and flow of the water. The woman burrowed her toes in the warm, wet sand.

All of a sudden, a single beam of light pierced the darkness. It came from the direction of the ocean, and a flashlight signaled back from the shore. Quick Morse-like flashes raced back and forth.

Did you see that, the woman asked.

Yes, said the professor.

What is it, asked the woman.

How would I know, answered the professor. I imagine they are fishermen.

The lights flashed on and off. The beam on the horizon glowed brightly, and it seemed to be gaining intensity and rapidly moving towards the island like a ball of fire. And then, abruptly, it went out. Large waves broke on the beach.

The woman got up, wishing to return to the motel. Her husband grumbled a bit, sighed, and slowly gathered himself up to go. Fishermen, he said faintly, as if talking to himself.

Arm in arm, they walked back to the room. The curtain and bedspread were of the same floral-patterned material, and the lamps gave off a dim light.

Too bad we didn't go to a better place, said the woman.

You wanted to be as close as possible to the ocean, answered the professor. This was the closest.

The sand had stuck to them, so they rinsed off under the tap in the sink.

Aren't you hungry, asked the professor.

I don't feel like going out tonight, said the woman.

Do you want to order in pizza, asked the professor. The woman shrugged her shoulders.

What toppings, he asked, and immediately added, The usual?

The usual, said the woman absentmindedly. She took a small notebook out of her handbag and started to add up columns of numbers.

Her husband phoned for the pizza.

We wasted too much money in New York, said the woman.

That's why we're eating pizza today, said the professor in an amused voice. Doesn't that make you feel young?

No, said his wife.

Muttering something, he propped two pillows behind his back, and flipped open a thick loose-leaf folder.

We'll go down to Key West tomorrow to see Hemingway's house, he said, determined to cheer his wife up.

She uttered an irritated laugh.

Those cats again, she said. You know I'm allergic to cats. We'll stay here tomorrow and spend the day on the beach . . .

The professor didn't answer. He put on his glasses, adjusted the lamp, and started to read. His wife picked up the motel's laminated instruction sheet and skimmed it over. There are two fire extinguishers in every hallway, she said.

Hmmm, mumbled the professor. He laid down the sheaf of papers, pulled some bills from his pocket, and held them out to his wife.

The pizza will be here any minute . . .

The woman took the bills and stared at the pile of papers on the bed.

Cervantes, she said, it's been thirty years already . . .

Hmmm, mumbled the professor again. He shifted to make himself more comfortable. And how many years have you been busy with your minerals?

That's not the same thing, said the woman. We discover new things every day . . .

New things are discovered in Cervantes too, said the professor. You're in a bad mood . . .

I don't know what's wrong with me, said the woman. I've gotten old all at once. Look at me.

You look fine, said her husband.

Outside a shrieking wind began to blow, and then another sound, like a heavy object being dropped.

Someone ran down the stairs. There were two knocks at the door. The woman yawned, counted the bills, and opened the door.

A young black man, dripping wet, burst into the room like a whirlwind.

Shhh. Shhh . . . he whispered sharply. No police, please, no police!

The professor looked up.

His wife stood still, petrified. The young man put his back up against the door and didn't move. His eyes darted around fearfully.

What's going on here, asked the professor. Who is that?

It's a robber, said the woman, a hint of gloating in her voice. Give him your wallet. Hurry!

Her husband held out his wallet hesitantly. The young man shook his head vigorously from side to side.

No, money, please, no police, no money . . .

The couple exchanged glances.

Are you sick, asked the woman.

No sick no sick, whispered the boy. The professor reached his hand out towards the phone, but the boy beat him to it and pulled the cord out.

No police, please . . . he begged. He was wearing shorts, a red tee-shirt, and was barefoot. A puddle was forming on the carpet beneath his feet.

Who are you, asked the professor. Everything happened so quickly that he didn't have the chance to get alarmed.

The young man wiped his face with his hand and pointed at the corridor as if gesturing towards the horizon.

Cuba, he whispered.

The couple stared at one another.

Are you a refugee from Cuba, asked the professor in Spanish.

The boy choked up and burst into tears. He began talking quickly. Someone had been waiting for them on the shore but a huge wave came . . . there were twenty of them . . . only he and another one could swim . . . the boat sank. Señor, Señora, por favor . . . the Coast Guard discovered them . . .

Twin rivulets of tears poured down his face.

Calm down, said the professor. He took a blanket and wrapped it around the young man.

The woman pursed her lips and remained silent. There was another knock on the door. The boy cringed in terror; the professor pushed him into the bathroom, threw a large towel over the puddle and glanced at his wife, as if asking for advice. She said it must be the pizza.

Have a nice evening, said the delivery guy.

Shut the door, ordered the professor. The woman put the pizza on the round table.

What do we do, she asked. She plugged in the telephone but didn't touch the handset.

Let me think, said her husband. He locked the door, fastened the door chain, and drew the curtains.

We have to notify the police, said the woman.

The professor didn't answer. He called the Cuban to come out of the bathroom.

Eat, he said, You must be hungry.

The young man nodded. They had been at sea for three days, with almost no food and water.

He took big bites of the crust, and the professor encouraged him to have another one, then sat on the carpet and ate a slice of pizza himself. The woman said she wasn't hungry.

They drank tap water because they decided not to leave the room. The boy sipped the water with his eyes closed.

I want a new life, he said.

The professor and his wife exchanged glances again.

We are only visitors here, said the woman, Tourists. We can't do anything illegal.

She spoke Spanish and the young man's eyes lit up.

Señora, please don't hand me over to the police, he said. He sent a beseeching look in the direction of the professor, who was toying with his glasses.

I have to think about this, he said. I need time to think.

A short while later they suddenly heard sounds of a commotion coming from downstairs. Breaks squealed, orders being given echoed down the hallways. Someone blew a whistle, doors slammed, people were running up and down the stairs.

The boy leaped up like a hunted animal. The blanket fell off his shoulders. The woman pressed her body against the wall while her husband surveyed the room feverishly. He motioned to the Cuban to lie on the bed, covered him from head to toe with the heavy bedspread, and placed two pillows and a suitcase on top. Don't breathe, he ordered him.

Coast Guard officers went from room to room. They showed their identification, apologized for the inconvenience, and informed the guests that they were in pursuit of illegal aliens who had infiltrated by sea. Anyone found harboring an illegal alien should be aware that the penalty is imprisonment, they said. The professor nodded. He gathered up the wet towel and blanket and said that they had just come back from the pool and hadn't seen anything. His wife remained silent. The officers came in, peeked into the bathroom, and apologized again.

Have a nice evening, they said.

You too, said the professor. He locked the door. Listened. Waited. Then he took the pillows and suitcase off the bed and lifted the bedspread. The young man lay there, as if dead.

You can get up now, he said.

The woman slowly drew up a chair and sat down. The Cuban murmured words of gratitude, and he was shaking so hard that the professor wrapped a blanket around him again and told him to keep quiet. Then he turned on the television. They stared at a tango dancing contest broadcast from Miami.

We must be insane, said the woman in Hebrew.

The professor didn't answer. He gathered his papers that had scattered all over the room.

My wife and I were born in Argentina, he told the young man. I teach Spanish Literature. He organized his folder.

I'm preparing a lecture on Cervantes, he added with a half-smile. Have you heard of Don Quixote?

You're crazy, said the woman.

Speak Spanish, if it's not too difficult for you, said the professor sarcastically, So everyone can understand. His wife looked at him in amazement.

Do you recognize what we've done? We've broken the law, she said.

I know, said the professor.

We're hiding an illegal alien in our room, said the woman.

I know, said the professor.

The boy tilted his head sideways, listening to the foreign language and suddenly said, with great longing, Don Quixote,

Don Quixote . . . He knelt before the woman and whispered, "O Princess Dulcinea . . ."

The woman retreated in panic.

"O Princess Dulcinea, lady of this captive heart, a grievous wrong hast thou done me to drive me forth with scorn, and with inexorable obduracy banish me from the presence of thy beauty. O lady, deign to hold in remembrance this heart, thy vassal, that thus in anguish pines for love of thee."

What is this, said the woman. She paled. The professor, on the other hand, looked astonished.

How do you know these quotations, he asked.

The young man said nothing, and the expression on his face softened as if pleasant memories had come to mind.

I grew up on Don Quixote, he said.

How is that so, wondered the professor.

Hold on, we have a problem to solve first, said the woman impatiently.

The boy seemed to be in shock. He sat hunched over on the carpet, and didn't answer.

I'm scared, I'm scared, he said finally.

Don't be scared, said the professor. We're thinking this through, right? My name is Ernest and this is my wife Amalia.

He held out his hand, and the young man grabbed it as if it were a lifesaver.

Miguel, he said. Then he bent over the chair hesitantly, and kissed the woman's hand.

I apologize for barging into your room, he said. I beg the lady's forgiveness.

The woman turned her head away but did not pull away her arm.

This is a nightmare, she said. We are insane. Her husband held the remote and turned up the volume.

Relax, don't panic, he requested, but he himself sounded frenzied. The Cuban looked heavenward.

"Fortune always leaves a door open in adversity in order to bring relief to it," he recited.

Ahh, rejoiced the professor. That is from chapter fifteen, "In Which Is Related The Unfortunate Adventure That Don Quixote Fell In With When He Fell Out With Certain Heartless Yanguesans"!

Are you a student of literature, he asked.

I don't believe this, said his wife. What is going on here?

The young man raked through his curly hair with his fingers and revealed shiny white teeth.

My grandfather worked in a cigar factory in Ybor City, in Tampa. That was a long time ago, in 1920 . . . he was a senior cigar roller and was treated with great respect . . . there was a man, El Lector, who would sit on a platform and read from the newspapers every day, also songs, and novels . . . my grandfather especially loved Don Quixote . . . he told us that this Lector had the voice of an opera singer, a thundering and joyous voice, and my grandfather, who sat close to him because of his seniority, learned every word by heart . . . my grandmother rolled cigars too . . . their daughter, my mother, they named Dulcinea . . . later there were hard times and they returned to Cuba . . . my grandfather missed the Lector and would talk of him all the time and because he didn't know how to read or write he asked my mother to read Cervantes aloud, and if she made a mistake he would correct her from memory, and so because of his enthusiasm my brothers and I learned all of Don Quixote by heart . . .

Unbelievable, said the professor. He looked at his wife as if to say, what do you think of all this? He urged the boy to continue his story. The woman started to get up but froze in place. A news flash was just being broadcast about a ship of Cuban migrants that had sunk off the shores of Islamorada. The Coast Guard was pulling bodies out of the water.

The young man hid his face in his hands.

We'll think of something, said the professor. He now had the wild-eyed look of someone who had just awakened from a restless sleep. He spread the floral-patterned blanket over the carpet in the corner of the room close to the bathroom, ordered the young man to lie down, and covered him.

Try and get some sleep; we'll take care of you . . . Miguel.

The boy burst into tears.

I want to go to Tampa, he said. I want to see the place that my grandfather talked about . . . I have the address of an old man from Cuba who lives there . . . they were friends . . .

He rolled down the top of his pants, struggled with an adhesive bandage on his stomach, and pulled out a crumpled piece of paper.

Here, he said.

The professor took the paper and studied it.

Hmm . . . he said. Okay. Go to sleep. We'll think of something.

Is Tampa far from here, asked the young man. Can I walk there?

Not on foot and not on horseback, ridiculed the woman.

The boy looked beseechingly at the professor.

"I'll bet that your worship thinks I have done something I ought not with my person," he quoted.

"It makes it worse to stir it, friend Sancho," whispered the professor with a weak smile.

"With this and other talk of the same sort master and man passed the night" . . . the Cuban immediately replied with the next sentence. His eyes were feverish and his mouth was dry. The professor gave him water to drink from a plastic cup and said, That's enough for now, get some rest. The young man lay his head down, exhausted, and immediately fell into a deep sleep.

The couple remained silent for a while.

Call the police, said the woman finally. Her husband remained silent.

We have to turn him in, she said. We're dealing with a stranger, an illegal alien. Apart from that he's a liar, I'm sure. It isn't possible that he memorized all of Don Quixote. I've never heard anything like it. Even you don't remember it all by heart. Who knows what else he's hiding from us.

People know the Bible by heart, said the professor.

Call before he wakes up, said the woman.

Her husband lay his folder down on the telephone.

No, he said decisively.

What do you mean no, said the woman. We have to turn him in. We're visitors here.

And if we were citizens, said the professor.

We would also have an obligation to turn him in.

Obligation can be defined in more ways than one, said the professor. He sat by the phone, as if guarding it.

I'm going crazy, said the woman. We're out of our minds. We'll sit in jail because of your stubbornness.

What do you suggest, asked the professor.

Turn him in. Now.

She moved towards the door but her husband blocked the way.

No, he said.

Call 911, hissed the woman angrily.

No, said the professor. Can you really turn him in? He called you Dulcinea and kissed your hand . . .

You're acting like Don Quixote yourself, you stupid old fool. Have you forgotten why we came here?

I haven't forgotten, said the professor. Look at him. Like a helpless baby.

Ahhh, said the woman. So that's what this is all about . . .

He's from Cuba, said the professor. You can't turn in a refugee from Cuba to the authorities. If they deport him his fate is sealed.

And what of our fate, said the woman.

They stood facing one another. The professor looked at his watch and pondered.

Ten fifteen, he said. At midnight we'll wake him up and take him to Tampa.

Over my dead body, said the woman.

Her husband didn't answer.

You hate me, said the woman.

I don't hate you, said the professor sadly. I love you, but somehow . . . you're always against me.

Outside the wind had died down. The woman threw herself on the bed and began to weep. The professor locked the suitcase. He turned off the lights, muted the television, and stared at the flickering screen as if looking at scenes from his life.

"There is no recollection which time does not put an end to, and no pain which death does not remove," he quoted his hero, mouthing the words quietly. And yet, here is this Cuban, living proof that there are some memories that time cannot erase . . . how strange and wonderful, he thought to himself.

At midnight he turned off the television, woke his wife up, and then gently shook the young man, whispering something in his ear. They left the room that was right at the end of the corridor, and hastily made their way down the flight of stairs like three shadows. The professor motioned the boy to lie on the back seat of the rental car, put the suitcase in the trunk, and made sure that his wife fastened her seatbelt. A single street-light illuminated the parking lot. He started the engine and drove quickly through the motel exit towards the boardwalk along the marina, and from there turned into the empty main thoroughfare. They drove north.

Are you okay, the professor asked his wife. She sat next to him with her eyes closed and didn't answer.

The boy lay on the back seat, curled up in the blanket he had brought with him. He was breathing heavily.

Too bad I didn't leave you then, when I had someone to leave with . . . too bad I didn't leave you, said the woman suddenly. A tremor went through the professor and he restlessly changed radio stations.

What a pity, what a pity about everything, he murmured. He drove silently, passing over bridges and along dusky shores and wetlands and from time to time turned the light on to glance at a map of Florida. Hours passed.

The professor stopped for gas once, bought a bottle of mineral water and sandwiches wrapped in cellophane. The young man slept.

Eat something, he said to his wife.

I want to throw up, said the woman.

The professor turned west, and to avoid the highway he drove down side roads and passed neighborhood after neighborhood with identical houses and shopping malls and deserted parking lots, and after awhile they reached a road that twisted through the dark swamps of the Everglades, and he doggedly continued without talking and without stopping again until daybreak obliterated the night fog. The single lane road widened, traffic picked up, and the tumultuous noise of the trucks passing by was deafening. They stopped at a traffic light.

The boy sat up, shaking off a nightmare, a deep wrinkle on his forehead as if he had aged in the hours that had passed while making their way to the western coast of the peninsula.

It's morning, said the professor. We'll be there soon. The Cuban stared dumbfounded at the Gulf of Mexico and the busy traffic. Downtown, impressive skyscrapers gleamed and the intersections and crosswalks teemed with people. The professor pulled over to the side, located a small street near 8th Avenue in Ybor City. He drove slowly, passing not far from the red brick buildings that were once bustling cigar factories and now housed restaurants, galleries, and night clubs, adorned with decorative lighting fixtures and flowering balconies.

Once the Tabaqueros used to live here, said the professor. He turned into an alley and stopped near a small house painted green.

This is it, said the professor. Number nine. He turned to the back seat, saying nothing.

The young man squeezed his eyes shut as if quickly running through the thoughts in his head.

We'll wait until you go in, said the professor. Don't tell a soul about us. If anyone asks you how you got here, say, I rode in on Rocinante, the famed steed of the Knight of the Sad Countenance . . .

The woman took an apple from her handbag and handed it to the young man.

Take care of yourself; it's a jungle out there, she said. You're in America, not Cuba . . .

The boy stepped out of the car and held the apple to his heart.

Go, said the professor.

He and his wife watched him until he disappeared into the open doorway of the house, embraced by a surprised old man. The professor rolled down the window and listened to the birds' Morning Prayer.

You're thinking what I'm thinking . . . said the woman.

Yes, said the professor.

Your Uncle Theo, the opera singer, said the woman.

The black sheep of the family, said the professor. He ran away from home but couldn't make a living from singing . . . .

El Lector, said the woman. He became the most famous lector in Tampa . . .

And most of all he loved Cervantes, said the professor.

At least it's obvious who you inherited that from, said the woman.

The professor smiled and pressed down on the gas pedal.

Where are we going, asked the woman.

I don't know, said the professor. Wherever you want, Amalia . . .

[The quotations from *Don Quixote De La Mancha* by Miguel De Cervantes were taken from the English translation by John Ormsby, 1885 (online version).]

◊ ~◆~ ◊

"A foreigner and a hired servant shall not eat thereof."

-    Exodus (Bible)

"Of a foreigner thou mayest exact it again . . ."

-    Deuteronomy (Bible)

◊ ~◆~ ◊

The Color of Cinnamon

Janice Eidus

On a July afternoon, in a colonial Mexican town high in the mountains, my five-year-old daughter, who's adopted from Guatemala, draws happily in a shaded corner of the patio of our Mexican *casa*. My husband and I bought this brightly-colored house six years ago. We're deeply attached to it, although we're here just a few months of each year. Our demanding jobs back home in New York City, where we live in an apartment approximately one-fifth the size of this house, preclude longer vacations. When we're not here, we keep the *casa* rented.

Across the large patio from my daughter, I sit lazily on a cushioned lounge chair, enjoying an occasional breeze, and listening to the sounds of the two chirping parakeets above me. We inherited the birds and their roomy, wicker cage when we purchased the *casa*. My daughter has re-named them: The blue parakeet is Budgie; the green one is Gudgie.

Common Boundary

I watch my daughter as she bends her head intently over her coloring book. Her long, black hair, loose and shimmering, falls across her heart-shaped face, and I note, not for the first time, how very much she resembles (far more than she resembles me) the sisters-in-law, *Señoras* Carmen and Silvia, who clean our *casa* and cook our meals. Like my daughter, the *Señoras* have skin the color of fresh cinnamon, and deep, black-brown eyes with long lashes, and shoulder-length hair that flows thick, black, and silky.

At the moment, the two *Señoras* are somewhere together in the *casa*, scrubbing and scouring, climbing and crawling, which they do unhesitatingly and without complaint every day. They do this for us when we're in town and for our renters throughout the year.

The two *Señoras* and my daughter could easily pass as family: Carmen, the grandmother; Silvia, the mother; my daughter, the grandchild and child. I am the Bronx-born Jew, fair-skinned and green-eyed, with ancestral roots not in Central America, but in Eastern Europe – the outsider, the *gringa* who doesn't belong.

Whenever I'm in Mexico, I find myself worrying that I've become a kind of contemporary domestic version of the 1920's "Fat Cat," minus top hat and cigar, plus gender change – *una imperialista, puerca, capitalista.* Despite my worries, I sit here, reveling in my laziness, as Budgie and Gudgie sweetly and noisily serenade me. I don't lift a finger to help the two *Señoras* clean my house.

If my Brooklyn-born, lower-middle-class parents – both avowed, life-long, left-wingers – were alive to see me today, they would be horrified. They, who raised me and my siblings in a wonderfully integrated, and diverse (sometimes dangerous) Bronx housing project, never wavered from their progressive social and political beliefs, which did not include ". . . hiring others to do our so-called 'dirty work,'" as my unfashionably-dressed, sensible-shoe wearing mother had declared one afternoon after we'd returned from an awkward, never-to-be-repeated visit to the opulent home of her suburban, Republican cousin, who employed a live-in maid, a gardener, and cook.

Expanding upon my mother's words, my always loud and didactic father said, with great feeling, "All work in one's home is noble and honest! Grow up," he looked hard at me and my sister and brother, although at me most of all, the sloppiest and most rebellious of the three of us, "and do all of your own work!"

Were he and my mother visiting me today in my Mexican *casa*, they also would bring up, with self-righteous passion, the fact that my daughter's ancestral history in

45

Guatemala very likely contains numerous sad, and enraging, stories of cinnamon-skinned women who did all sorts of ". . . so-called 'dirty work'" for low – or no – pay, and who were horrifically exploited by unfeeling, imperialistic *gringos* and *gringas* who very much resemble me.

My parents would be right, of course. But, here's my dilemma: I hate doing housework. And so, despite my own progressive social and political beliefs, I can't stop myself from taking advantage of the fact that, here in Mexico, I can afford to pay someone else to do it for me.

As a child, back in the Bronx, in our claustrophobically small kitchen in the housing project, day after day, I watched my mother as she swept, dusted, washed, and wiped, while my father, despite his rhetoric about "noble, honorable work," never once lifted a finger to help her do what to him was "women's work," and, therefore, beneath him. I swore to myself, like so many rebellious daughters before me, that I would grow up to be *nothing* like my mother. I assured myself that such pointless, trivial, domestic tasks were beneath me, too.

I was wrong, of course. As an adult, I quickly discovered what the point was of all that seemingly endless sweeping, mopping, washing, and dusting: Living amidst filth is disgusting. Women's work or not, I didn't want to live surrounded by clutter, *schmutz*, and all the vermin that *schmutz* attracts. Fairly quickly, I came to see that there's nothing intrinsically demeaning about taking care of one's home, and that, in fact, housework really *is* honest and noble work.

But, I still loathe doing it. I find it to be maddeningly boring, repetitious, and uninspiring. I'd rather do anything else: grade student papers; alphabetize my books; comfort a chronically whiney and depressed friend.

Therefore, for two fabulous months each year, I do no housework at all. *Señoras* Carmen and Silvia sometimes laughingly tease me, speaking slowly because they know how primitive my Spanish is: "*Señora* Janice, we don't believe that you know how to boil water or sweep a floor!"

In my grammatically-flawed Spanish, I laughingly respond that, "*En mi casa en Nueva York*," I do both of these tasks, plus more. "But not," I add honestly, "as well as you do them, *Señoras!*"

Casting their eyes to the floor, they shyly and graciously accept my compliment, and then they tell me how glad they are to be in my employ. "*Mucho gusto, Señora* Janice," they smile. Silvia adds that it is the money she earns working for me that enables her to send her son to college, a dream she never thought would come true.

Now it's my turn to cast my eyes downward, embarrassed by the power imbalance in our relationship.

"Mama!" my daughter suddenly exclaims from across the patio, breaking my train of thought. She puts down her coloring book and crayons and comes to stand beside me.

"Yes, sweetheart?" I shade my eyes and look directly into her dark eyes, amazed, as I so often am, by the absolute ferocity of my love for her.

"I want to go help Silvia and Carmen," she says.

"*Seguro*," I say, nodding, speaking in my stilted Spanish, trying as best as I can, in my Jewish, *gringa* way, to keep her connected to the language of her birth country.

She turns from me and happily skips through the sliding glass door that separates the patio from the rest of the *casa*, in order to join the two *Señoras*, who are, by now, probably cleaning the master bedroom, dusting the lamps, sweeping beneath the queen-sized bed, plumping the pillows and straightening the rose-colored, embroidered bedspread, all the while talking nonstop to each other about their family's woes and joys, as they always do while working.

This isn't the first time that my daughter has helped the *Señoras* do their work. They've been showing her how to grill *tortillas con queso*, and how to clean silver so that it shines like the moon. "*La luna*," she eagerly repeats, staring into the *Señoras'* eyes, waiting for their approval, which they give freely to her, along with *mucho* hugs and kisses.

Now, alone on the terracotta-colored patio, listening to the songs of Budgie and Gudgie, I sink even more deeply and lazily into the soft, cushioned lounge chair, happy to know that these strong women who look so much like her, and who speak her birth language, are in my daughter's life.

A delightful warm breeze ruffles my hair, and I close my eyes, envisioning my daughter all grown up, a high-powered, twenty-something businesswoman, living in a spacious, elegant Park Avenue apartment kept pristine and perfectly ordered by numerous housekeepers and assistants of various ethnicities and backgrounds.

In a flash, the image changes, and I see her as a hard-working preschool teacher, living in a cramped, walk-up studio in downtown Brooklyn, a studio that she loves in all its cluttered, messy, dusty chaos.

Common Boundary

A new image: Here she is in the same small studio, but this time it's pristine and meticulous, kept that way by no one but herself, a young woman who finds housework soothing and fulfilling.

But, wait: She's older now, in her forties. She has returned to her roots in Central America, perhaps to her birth country of Guatemala, or to our house in Mexico, where she is now the *Señora* in charge, the owner of this colorful, grand house, which is kept in tip-top shape by a couple of hard-working, cinnamon-skinned *Señoras* who very much resemble Carmen and Silvia.

At last, I open my eyes and rise slowly from the comfort of my chair. As I head inside the house, I promise myself that, whichever path my daughter chooses to take, I will be happy for her, knowing that, in housework and all things, she has found a way to be herself. I also promise myself that, right now, I will make myself a delicious lunch of scrambled eggs and *tortillas*, with no help at all from the cinnamon-skinned *Señoras*.

The Plain Brown Envelopes

Mitch Levenberg

Ours was a long journey home. First there was the ride to the airport. Jack, our facilitator in Guangzhou, was meeting us in the lobby of the White Swan at 8 A.M., but which side of the lobby? He said the side in which we all received our babies' visas from him, sealed with all our paperwork in a brown envelope that was not to be opened until we arrived in New York, and only then by an immigration inspector. I feared the gum which sealed the envelope was already drying up, clinging to life. Then there was that part of me I still didn't quite trust, who wanted to open the envelope now, who wanted to open anything and everything he was told not to open. Yes, but the envelope seemed to be opening just a bit at the edges. I felt, perhaps, we should reseal it, lick it again, or put scotch tape on it, but no doubt that would be as bad as opening it, since the implication of resealing it was that it had been opened. Was this the start of everything beginning to unravel?

Common Boundary

There were so many elevators and entrances and exits. And there were new faces all the time: pot-bellied midwesterners, sleek Asian business women – holding slim black bags which seemed to hold nothing but its own internal self. We were anything but sleek. We were bloated by luggage, bags hanging from bags, our past entangled with our future. The baby now seemed more curious than cranky, giving us one final chance to get her out of here, saying nothing, making no indication of being unhappy.

Jack was late. I walked over to the other side of the lobby to see if he was there and on the way met Maryanne and Hillel, a couple from our adoption group, who were staying one more day. They were both in swimsuits on their way to the pool. There always seemed to be a relentless straining on their part to avoid the fact they were in China with a Chinese baby. They could just as well have been going out to the pool in Miami or Vegas. "We're leaving," I told them. "We're staying another day," Maryanne said. "Lucky you," I said. They looked at me strangely, unsure whether I was kidding or not. I wasn't kidding. "We have to stay one more day," Maryanne said. "Part of our package deal." Their baby was asleep in the stroller. When I came back to where my wife and baby stood, there was still no sign of Jack. I walked out of the lobby and into the street. Vans lined the parking lot ready to transport the babies and their new parents away, out of here, to New England, the Great Plains, California, Texas, Newark, New Jersey, Holland – little Chinese babies sprinkled everywhere, depending on plain brown envelopes already beginning to unseal. How strong could these envelopes be? How much could they really contain before bursting, bursting before the immigration official could open them himself? Certainly they had a time limit. You can't expect to put your life and your child's life in a plain brown envelope and expect it to hold together very long. Gum is gum. They might as well have put the baby inside the envelope and sealed it until we got to New York.

So we waited for Jack as we had waited for that cab the night we left Brooklyn, and I wondered if perhaps Jack would never show up at all and we'd miss our plane and all the connections afterwards, and it might just be too difficult to reschedule, to depend on the brown envelope to remain closed even longer; and the longer we waited the more I could swear I heard the mouth of the envelope begin to groan, slowly at first, then protractedly, angrily, like an iceberg cracking open, and I was about to panic until I heard my wife say, "There he is!" almost the exact same way she said, "There she is!" when my daughter came out of the hotel room.

Common Boundary

It was Jack still wearing the same New York Yankees baseball cap. He came over to us and said, "Sorry I'm late," and then took our luggage, everything, really, except the baby and the brown envelope, which, when I looked at it again, hadn't really opened anymore than the day before.

We piled into a white van and Jack drove erratically through Guongzhou morning traffic. There was the herky, jerky motion of traffic here like a kind of subtle impatience or restlessness, not quite yet full blown – old men on bicycles still naturally rode into intersections, cut off traffic, not even looking at cars, as if they didn't really exist or shouldn't have, and would be quite willing to die if they had to, as if they were too programmed to act any other way, as if death wasn't nearly as bad as change. On the other side, they seemed out of place, a creeping anachronism, tolerated by the cars and vans and buses, all flexing their own muscles now, stretching themselves out so that even the one lane reserved for bicycles seemed in danger of annihilation, or at the very least of serious sideswiping.

One old man on a bike suddenly, though deliberately, turned his way into the intersection, passing in front of us as if we might have been some curiosity, some harmless fauna that found itself in the middle of the road, and that it was more as if we had suddenly appeared in front of the old man than he suddenly appeared before us. As he was making his turn, I noticed him stare into the van, for just an instant, but long enough to upset the careful precision and timing needed to make the turn without Jack running him over.   In other words, he was allowed to make his turn, but nothing else. He couldn't look at, nor think about, anything else. This was forbidden.   It was understood tacitly, on all sides, that anything but making this turn was not allowed, that he was barely allowed to exist in order to make that turn let alone to look, not at, but into the van he was passing, to look at and then think about its contents, to upset a fragile alliance between the old and new, to risk his life, our lives, perhaps China itself.

Jack, in his own mind, would have every right to kill the old man. I will never forget his face, no matter how short a time I saw it because it looked at our daughter in a way that we never could, that told of ancient bloodlines and loyalties and betrayals that we could never understand. All the old man knew was that we were taking part of that out of China, draining it of its youth, about to corrupt it with Western ideas and culture, the new modernism which was destroying him as well.

Something had moved inside the old man. Yet, ironically, outside there was this perfect stillness as if he no longer moved at all, as if all motion had stopped. Something had awoken that had perhaps lain dormant for ages, something beyond his control, so that the fact the van had only slowed slightly, that although Jack caught the old man slowing down just in time to slow the speed of the car, he could not stop. Jack needed to move forward, perhaps even to risk a collision in front in order to avoid the unthinkable collision from behind. This all took place just for an instant, mind you; if you blinked you'd never know the man was there at all, was staring so intently at our daughter and at us. Yet I think I remember that face very well. Of course, as I think back it could be a conglomeration of many faces, of all the faces of all the old men and women riding their bicycles that morning, all of them looking curiously and then disapprovingly and then resignedly at us.

Then Jack blew his horn at him, and its raw and urgent sound seemed to bring the old man back to his own tragic and deliberate motion, jolted him out of his perfect trance and nearly made him stumble off the bike. Yes, the old man moved now towards a future wrought with oblivion as we headed, we believed (for the moment we passed the old man, or did he pass us?) towards a future of hope and promise.

Into the Light: Safe Haven 1944

Ruth Sabath Rosenthal

> And you that shall cross from shore to shore
> years hence are more to me,
> and more in my meditations, than you might suppose.
> - Walt Whitman, *Crossing Brooklyn Ferry*

Thank God for you, *Henry Gibbins*,

ship of dreams laden with bedraggled brethren

dark and fair, tall and short,

frail-boned and gaunt, each and every one a survivor

reborn in the wake of conscience.

Blessed, their leader, Ruth Gruber,

praised, her leader, Franklin D. Roosevelt;

and you, Captain Korn, your kind face and outstretched arms,

your smiling crew, their helpful hands,

your great vessel's stalwart bulk, hallowed halls, glistening

white toilets, your sky-crowned decks

surrounded by sea-speckled rail—a far cry

from barbed wire.

Common Boundary

Divine are you, clean fresh air that fills sunken chests,

lungs ashen from the fires of Auschwitz-Birkenau,

Bergen-Belsen, Buchenwald, Dachau, Treblinka.

And you, buoyant sea, revered for strong currents, changing

tides, gulls that glide the breeze and assuage wounded spirit;

and you, dining halls bejeweled with vegetables,

cornucopia of meats, kaleidoscope of sweets that swell

shrunken bellies, smooth withered souls—

"Are you America?" each wary sojourner asks.

Soft pillows and ample blankets nestled

in vast tiers of bunks, nightmares you help smother,

sweet dreams you set in motion;

talent shows, chess tournaments, movies,

"Are you?"

Oh, most wondrous throng—my ancestry—

it is *you* who are America, *my* America!

~

Author's note on "Into the Light: Safe Haven 1944"

The *Henry Gibbins* was a U.S. army transport ship sailing within a naval convoy that transported these 982 "most needy" holocaust survivors over the waters of war-ravaged

Europe, German air-fire besieging the convoy en route to America and the Isle of Manhattan, N.Y. July 1944. The exodus, arranged by President Franklin D. Roosevelt and carried out by Ruth Gruber on behalf of the United States government, was aptly named "Operation Safe Haven."

It was on August 3, 1944, that the Henry Gibbins sailed through N.Y. Harbor, dazed refugees bedazzled by the Statue of Liberty and the Manhattan skyline – not a dry eye on the ship.

The sojourn, from unimaginable enslavement and tyranny to safety, continued by railroad to Oswego, N.Y. and the army base Ft. Ontario, which had been converted to a refugee camp for these home-less, country-less people. The bedraggled group arrived at the fort August 5, 1944 and, for eighteen months, lived there tending their wounds and immersing themselves in the process of healing and preparing to move into homes and apartments across America (or any country of their choice that had offered to welcome them).

Today, the site of Ft. Ontario serves as a memorial to these survivors; the administration building, renamed "Safe Haven Museum and Education Center," houses priceless photographs and documents mapping what truly was an extraordinary exodus out of darkness into the light.

◊ ~◆~ ◊

"Voyage, travel, and change of place impart vigour."

- Seneca

". . . For this great journey.
What did this vanity
But minister communication of
A most poor issue?"

- William Shakespeare (*Henry VIII*)

◊ ~◆~ ◊

They Set Sail in Springtime

Excerpt from *Mortal Love* (novel)

Rivka Keren

Translated from the Hebrew by Yael Politis

A gull alights near the girl. She eyes it suspiciously, in all its particulars, eye, beak, small head tilted back, wings limp at its side. Give it a crumb, they tell her. She remains silent, bracing herself in a wide-legged stance, licking the salt from her lips. Would a seagull with no beak still be a seagull? Is a gull that has no eye, no head, no wing still a gull? The people lounge about the deck next to one another, spent from the tribulations of the storm, yet uncommonly attentive, and the pale white light lends them the guise of large wax dummies. Give it a crumb, they say to the girl, give it . . . a sudden swell tosses the ship from side to side. The girl, falling and quickly rising up in retreat, mingles in with the other refugees, some of whom have begun to vomit and some of whom are praying, and seats herself next to a consumptive-looking man

with glowing eyes who says to her, Come here Edit, hold tight
to my hand; and she scowls, reluctantly obeying her father's
wishes, saying, A seagull. It's good to see a gull, he says, It's a
sign that we must be near shore, any time now we might hear
the sailor up in the crow's nest calling out, Land ahoy! Do
you remember the story I told you about Columbus? he asks,
and the girl tenses: Columbus is a lethal name; from
Columbus Street in Budapest there was no view of the sea and
the sidewalks were strewn with the dying. A seagull means
land, the man repeats, looking at his daughter the way one
examines a wound, and her mouth is contorted as she says,
But Pappa, there have been seagulls the whole way, yesterday
and the day before, the whole time we've been at sea there
have been flocks of seagulls, didn't you notice them? The
man takes his hand away from his daughter's to draw a
crushed match box from his pocket, one of many that he
keeps in a secret collection, brings the box to his nose,
sneezes, rubs his nostrils, and repeats this ritual over and over;
the bitter addicting fragrance of tobacco for a moment
prevails over the stench of seaweed and vomit, causing those
nearby to turn their heads and sigh, for they have long ago
finished the last of the cigarettes they were given in Italy and
can only dream of a smoke, the way the girl dreams of the
round caraway-studded rolls her mother used to give her each

morning, when Columbus was still just Columbus and gulls were just sea birds, and dreams were comforting companions, rather than omens of destruction.

The horizon rises and falls, the deck is washed with foam, and the gull clings to the rail, fluttering and emitting a loud screech. The man dozes off. The girl, the bird, and the sea are swallowed in haze. The question is: who will outsmart whom? Since the girl has learned that the sea in daylight is not at all like the sea in the dark of night, she diligently remains awake to protect her father from the evil spirits pretending to be fish and birds. Is a headless gull still a gull, or some kind of monster that has had its head wrung off, she wonders. With her hands? . . . . With a shoelace? . . . With the cable of the fire extinguisher? . . . She peeks out from under lowered lashes, makes a slight movement, bends over. Will it be gone by the time she's done counting the winged snakes that float in the water? Will it be gone by the time she finishes whispering the words? She faces the bird. Her hand reaches out slowly and the gull gives her a glassy stare, Yes, that's that look that she can't bear. Count the snakes! . . . Whisper the words! . . . Quickly . . . quickly . . . Hey, mister, what's your daughter doing over there?! They waken the man and insist, Look, look at her! The child is torturing that poor bird! *Te*, Edit, he says, numb with sleep, What are you doing, come, here. But the child remains out of his reach, leaning against the railing. Up for a moment, down for a moment, if she is tempted into looking there, even a glance, it will be the end of her, so she mustn't look into the water. I'm not doing anything, she says, and her father gathers himself to stand on feeble legs, What does he care about all these people, people who go sticking their nose in where it doesn't belong, thinking they're such do-gooders, but when it comes to themselves . . . they can all go to hell, bunch of hypocrites, hasn't it been enough, all that he's been through, now he has to suffer through the punishment of rocking along in this rusty tub, humiliated, lacking any kind of privacy, facing an elusive future the mere contemplation of which is entirely dispiriting. Come to sleep, he says to the girl, taking her hand and walking toward their large, densely populated cabin. But the stormy sea off Crete keeps all but a few of them awake, and so the unshaven man whose ill-fitting clothes hang as if his body were a crooked hanger and his close-faced daughter also remain awake, counting the blows of the waves against the hull of the ship. I don't feel good, says the girl and her father replies, Neither do I, no one does, but it's easier for children, you'll soon fall asleep; and the girl begs him to tell her a story, stretching out on her bottom bunk, closing her eyes, and envisioning an expanse of land, golden with light, a blinding wasteland, and says, Tell me the story about the Foreign Legion soldier in the Sahara Desert; and the man clears the phlegm from his throat, gagging whenever he speaks or swallows. What had she been doing up there on the deck while he napped, What had she . . . the child stares at him impatiently and whispers, *Na?*, and he gives in and begins telling the story, slowly, about the fortress of sands out in the middle of nowhere and the lamentations of the dead soldier who has been drawn back to it by his great yearning for the sheikh's beautiful daughter, and the child awaits the story's ending, the part where the soldier springs back to life at the touch of his faithful beloved's hand, and when the end finally arrives, in an increasingly hoarse voice, it is swallowed up in the general buzz of chatter. To feel contempt for this vitality surrounding them is to feel contempt for one's own existence; but the girl hates these people, whose voices, movements, and belongings invade her soul, and she prays for them all to vanish and leave her alone with her father, for if she doesn't remind him to wash and to get up to walk a bit, who will? And if she doesn't protect him from the onslaughts of tears, the fits of depression, and his dangerous games with fire, who will? Who will comfort him? Who will watch out for the monsters? So she must remain on her constant alert, lest a moment's distraction brings irreparable disaster down upon them.

So the girl thanks her father for the story and instructs him to lie down to sleep, and he obediently rises to move over to his own nearby bunk, saying, You feel better now, don't you, my little flower? She replies that she does and watches him once again take out the crushed match box, sniff a pinch of tobacco, and sneeze, and the people around them say, *Gesundheit*, peering at him curiously as if they had been waiting for just such an opportunity, for what's-his-name, the aloof Hungarian refugee to sneeze and finally give them the chance indirectly to enter into casual conversation with him; but the man makes no reply, wiping his nose and staring at the creaking floor, and hoarsely saying, Good night Editke, and the girl's hostile glare scathes the busybodies stretched out on their pallets, limbs asunder, and she says, Good night, Pappa, try not to let all this noise bother you.

~

. . . . No matter how hard she tries she cannot imagine what Jerusalem must be like, much less her unknown relatives, and she begins to cry in the contained way she has acquired at the convent: the tears flow inward, her lips are pursed, her hands balled up into fists, yes, like that. The girl's hand chances on a loose nail, pulls it out, and violently scratches lines, left and right, and in the morning the baldheaded woman in the upper bunk will complain that her bed is covered with crosses, and will train a meaningful stare on the unfriendly little sneak of a girl who always wears a scowl on her face, as if the world owes her something; she should be grateful she's still alive and go play with the other children instead of clinging to her father's behind. Yesterday the seagull and now this, she will say in an outraged voice, but the cabin walls are anyway covered with scribbles and scratches, and no one will pay the least attention to her, at most they will nod their heads, Yes, she is a peculiar child. And they will conspire to ignore the mysterious crosses the same way they had ignored what had happened with the bird and all the other strange goings-on during this journey, for they know they can count on trouble to come looking for them, and have no desire to make a special effort to rush out to meet it.

The ship is overloaded and the storm hammers at it, causing it to list between the waves of water, their color as dark as that of the ink in the glass inkwell that the little girl had found in the rubble that remained of their home after the war. The windows of the apartment that looked out over the rusty remains of the Chain Bridge were broken and on the floor were heaps of clothing, knickknacks, tattered books, a bottle of perfume that somehow managed to survive intact, and slivers of what had once been her father's violin. The brass plate bearing the name Gottzeit remained fixed to the front entrance, in the closet was an address book neatly filled with the names of the dead, and on the bathroom floor lay a filthy towel which her father clutched up, blowing his nose into it, and broke into a fitful bleating, broken, like the horn of a sinking ship, ah . . . ahhhh . . . Had the ship sounded its horn? The girl stops scraping and scratching, huddled up against the wall, alert.

The wooden planks creak. An empty bottle rolls from side to side. People call out in their sleep. An iron door opens and slams shut and the girl, like Jonah being swallowed up by the whale, is swept out into the abyss and tossed upward, wondering in terror if she will ever again feel the comfort of solid ground beneath her feet, and she casts a worried frown at the nearby bunk and sees her father sitting there trembling, and she goes over to him whispering, *Apu!* He gestures for her to sit at his side, puts his arm about her, and says, You will stay with me, you won't leave me; his teeth are clacking together, and she replies, No, I won't leave you, Pappa, concealing the nail in the palm of her hand. There had been a few orphaned nails left sticking out of the walls of their home. Here was where the picture of Grandma and Grandpa had hung, and here the portrait of Chatam Sofer, and here had been the needlework picture that Mamma made, You remember, Rebecca and Eliezer by the well, and over there was a reproduction of the painting by Szinyei-Merse Pál, that wonderful carefree picnic on the slope of a hill, *Majális*, yes, that's what it was called, May Festival, and here were the sketches given to us by Mar . . . Mar . . . and the name she couldn't bring herself to speak stuck in her father's throat as well. The oath you took, Edit, said the voice, The oath, and the terror silenced her, while her father went on rambling from nail to nail, crumpling the towel, whimpering, and gathering up the charred remains of the parquet floor upon which the Russians had lit their fires during the battles; Look what I found, he said back then, and she looked over and saw all of them together, as if they were still alive, looking straight into the distant lens of the camera.

Morning dawns on a tranquil day and the deck is crowded with people singing *"Hatikvah,"* their faces eastward, like sunflowers seeking rays of light, and the girl lingers behind, taking refuge in the still dimness of the cabin, all of its occupants, apart from her father, having abandoned it, and she rearranges her pathetic belongings for the umpteenth time: the armless blonde doll, the almost toothless comb, a page from an old collection of stories, "The Girl Who Turned Into a Pea," a petrified square of chocolate, the stub of a pencil, a spoon, the string of a violin, clothes that are too small for her, a cloth pouch tied with a ribbon. The girl asks nothing and her father remains silent. He absentmindedly pulls at the hair on his legs, sniffs tobacco, passes matches from one box to another, laughs, and sighs. They had risen at sunrise, stood a long while in line for the use of the faucet, skillfully avoided the puddles of vomit, drank bitter tea, then checked one another's throats, tongues, teeth, and the girl declared her father's temperature normal. He, to his dismay, discovered two lice in her hair. One word buzzed from mouth to ear: Tonight.

The ship did drop anchor in the dark. Lights flickered on the shoreline. Orders. A tremendous commotion. Shadows climbing a rope ladder . . . the British are nowhere in sight . . . Hurry . . . they are lowered into the lifeboats. The rocking of the boat, the slap of a wave, the girl huddles in her father's lap, burying her face in his shirt. You have to watch out for the monsters in the water . . . What were the words her brother had taught her to whisper? Let's imagine she is sitting on the swing in the park above the carpet of linden flowers and her mother tells the boys to take turns pushing her, and the three of them fling her up and down, up and down, E-dit, E-dit, and then they go for ice cream, licking industriously, first around the edges, then the top, then biting a tiny hole in the bottom of the cone to suck out the last drop of vanilla, and finally devouring the entire cone, nibbling away . . . and finally devouring the entire cone . . . and finally devouring . . . and finally . . .

◊ ~◆~ ◊

"We talk of human life as a journey; but how variously is that journey performed!"

-   Rev. Sydney Smith

"I am not the native of a small corner only; the whole world is my fatherland."

-   Seneca

◊ ~◆~ ◊

Wooden Trunk from Buchenwald

John Guzlowski

When my parents, my sister, and I finally left the refugee camp in Germany after the war, we were allowed to bring very little, only what would fit into a steamer trunk. The problem was that we couldn't afford to buy one. Not many of the families living in the camps could. You can imagine why that was, so my father did what other people did. He and a friend got together and built a trunk.

Someplace, somehow, they found a hammer and a saw and nails and some metal stripping, and they set to work. Getting the wood wasn't a problem. They got the wood from the walls of the barracks they were living in. It was one of the old German concentration camps that had been converted to living space for the refugees, the Displaced Persons, and this place didn't have finished walls of plaster, or anything like that. If you wanted a board, you could just pull it off of the wall, and that's what my father did.

I don't think he felt guilty about busting up those walls. He had spent enough time staring at them, so that he probably felt he could do anything he wanted to them, and it would be okay. I think if a man spends enough time staring at a thing, finally it becomes his by a kind of default. I don't know if that's what my dad thought. He didn't say a lot about building that wooden trunk, and he probably didn't give it much thought.

The trunk my father and his friend built out of those old boards wasn't big. It was maybe four feet wide and three feet tall and three feet deep. The walls of the trunk were about 3/4 of an inch thick. But wood is always heavy, so that even though it wasn't that big, that trunk generally needed two people to lift it. My father, of course, could lift it by himself. He was a small man, a little more than five feet tall, but he had survived four years in Buchenwald as a slave laborer. That work taught him to do just about any work a man could ask him to do. My father could dig for beets in frozen mud and drag fallen trees without bread or hope.

My parents couldn't get much into the trunk, but they put into it what they thought they would need in America and what they didn't want to leave in Germany: some letters from Poland, four pillows made of goose feathers, a black skillet, some photographs of their time in Germany, a wooden cross, some clothing, of course, and wool sweaters that my mother knitted for us in case it was cold in America. Somewhere, I've got a picture of me wearing one of those sweaters. It looks pretty good. My mother knitted it before her eyes went bad, and she was able to put little reindeer and stars all over that sweater.

When we finally got to America, my parents didn't trash that wooden trunk or break it up, even though there were times when breaking it up and using the wood for a fire would have been a good idea to keep us warm. Instead, they kept it handy for every move they made in the next forty years. They carried it with them when we had to go to the migrant farmers' camp in upstate New York where we worked off the cost of our passage to America. And my parents carried it to Chicago, too, when they heard from their friend Wenglaz that Chicago was a good place for DPs, for refugees. And they carried that trunk to all the rooming houses and apartment buildings and houses that we occupied in Chicago. I remember in those early days in Chicago that there were times when the only things we owned were the things my mother and father brought with us in that trunk, and the only furniture we had was that trunk. Sometimes it was a table, and sometimes it was a bench, and sometimes it was even a bed for my sister and me.

When we were kids growing up, my sister Donna and I played with the trunk. It had large block letters printed on it, the names of the town we came from in Germany, the port we sailed from, and the port we sailed to in America. We would trace the letters with our fingers even before we could read what they said. We imagined that trunk was the boat that brought us to America, and we imagined that it was an airplane and a house. We even imagined that it was a swimming pool, although this got harder to imagine as we got older and bigger.

When my parents retired in 1990 and moved from Chicago to Sun City, Arizona, they carried that trunk with them. That surprised me because they didn't take much with them when they went to Arizona. They sold or gave away almost everything that they owned, almost everything that they had accumulated in thirty-eight years of living in America. They got rid of bedroom suites and dining room suites, refrigerators and washing machines, ladders and lawnmowers. My parents were never sentimental, and they didn't put much stock in stuff. They figured it would be easier to buy new tables and couches when they got to Sun City.

But they kept that trunk and the things they could put in it.

And a TV set.

After my father died in 1997, my mother stayed on in Arizona. She still had the trunk when she died. She kept it in a small, 8 foot x 8 foot utility room off the carport. My parents had tried to pretty it up at some point during their time in Arizona. The original trunk was bare, unpainted wood, and was covered with those big, blocky, white letters I mentioned. But for some reason, my parents had painted the wooden trunk, painted it a sort of dark brown, almost a maroon color; and they had papered the bare wood on the inside of the trunk with wallpaper, a light beige color with little blue flowers.

When my mom died, I was with her. Her dying was long and hard. She had had a stroke and couldn't talk or understand what was said. She couldn't move at all either. When she finally died, I had to make sense of her things. I contacted a real estate agent, and he told me how I could get in touch with a company that would sell off all of my mother's things in an estate sale.

I thought about taking the wooden trunk back home with me to Valdosta, Georgia. I thought about all it meant to my parents and to me, how long it had been with them. How they had carried it with them from the DP camps in Germany to Sun City, Arizona, this desert place so different from anything they had ever known overseas. I knew my sister

Donna didn't want the trunk. I called her up, and we talked about the things my mother left behind and the estate sale and the trunk. Donna has spent a lifetime trying to forget the time in the DP camps and what the years in the slave labor camps during the war had cost my parents. But did I want it?

I contacted UPS about shipping it, what it would cost, how I would have to prepare the trunk. They told me it would cost about $150 to ship. But did I want it?

I finally decided to leave it there and to let it get sold off at the estate sale. That wooden trunk had been painted over, and the person buying it wouldn't know anything about what it was and how it got there. It would just be an anonymous, rough-made trunk, painted a dark brown, almost maroon color with some goofy wallpaper inside.

Thinking back on all of this now, I'm not sure I know why I left that trunk there. When I'm doing a poetry reading and tell people the story of the trunk and read one of my poems about it, people ask me why I left it. It doesn't make any kind of sense to them. And I'm not sure now that it makes any kind of sense to me either. Why did I leave it?

I was pretty much used up by my mom's dying. It had been hard. My mother went into the hospital for a gall bladder operation and had had that stroke, and the stroke left her paralyzed, confused, and weak. She couldn't talk or move, and the doctor told me that my mother couldn't even understand what was being said to her.

Her condition got worse, and I put her in a hospice in Sun City. I sat with her there for three weeks, watched her breathing get more and more still. Sometimes, her eyes would open, and she would look around. I would talk to her about things I remembered, her life and my father's life, my life and my sister's life. I don't know if she understood anything. She couldn't blink or nod, or make sounds with her mouth. I just talked to her about what I remembered, any stupid thing, the bus rides we took, the TV shows she always watched, the oleanders she and my dad liked to grow and plant in the backyard. I didn't think that there was much else I could do for her.

When she died, I didn't want to do anything except get back home to my wife Linda in Georgia. Maybe the extra burden of figuring out how to carry that trunk back to Georgia was more than I could deal with. Or maybe I thought that trunk wasn't the same trunk that my parents had brought from the concentration camp in Germany. It had been painted, changed. Or maybe I just wanted that trunk to slip away into memory the way my mother had slipped away, become a part of my memory, always there but not there.

◊ ~◆~ ◊

"Diogenes, when asked from what country he came, replied,
'I am a citizen of the world.'"

\-   Diogenes Laertius

". . . there is no journey but hath its end."

\-   Montaigne

◊ ~◆~ ◊

Cheekago

Dagmara J. Kurcz

My mom is not the kind of mom you would want to take to your school or the playground and show off, like some kids do with their mothers. She is not color blind, but chooses to wear brightly colored outfits that remind me of the eighties shows like *Dynasty* and *Miami Vice*. And although we are in the States for only a month and she doesn't speak much English, she mixes Polish with some American words she'd learned from other people who don't know anything about the English language, but think they do. She says stuff like: "We need to 'wyrentowac' an apartment." Notice the word "rent" in the middle of the Polonized version of the word. Or she buys "orange juisa," and "Christmoos" decorations, although there isn't an "oo" sound in the original word. And what she really wants is to live in a house that has many "floory," "drivewaya" and a big "yarda."

I hear her talking on a phone and figure she's speaking with my cousin Jack. When she's finished, she passes me the receiver, and Jack asks me if mom is spending a lot of time with "the Americans."

"Sure," I say, "if by Americans you mean the Poles who occupy the three levels of the house we're renting, then yes."

On the other line Jack tells me stuff about grandma, how she cries all the time because she hates being alone. So I make up some excuse and hang up the phone. I don't want him to know I'm crying, but I know that once the tears start falling, my voice breaks and everyone always knows that I'm tearing up, even if they're on another continent.

My mom cries too, mostly because of her job. She's cleaning houses in a cleaning service, and it's August and she sweats a lot. This one lady told her supervisor once that my mom "stinks," and the supervisor told mom to make sure she takes daily showers. For the next week mom cried every evening, not even trying to hide it. So she's looking for another job, something that doesn't require scrubbing other people's toilets.

The job search takes forever if you don't know the language, the streets, and are unable to read maps, which mom tells me is a women's thing, and I wonder how women ever get anywhere on their own. Most of the time mom finds ads in *Dziennik Związkowy* – a Polish newspaper, and decides to check them out. After consulting with neighbors about street directions, she takes our neighbor Basia, who also wants a job, and me because I know the most English out of the three of us, and we're off to some unknown location, hoping to find something better.

So here we are, on our way to pick up a guy who promised to hire my mom and Basia in a school cafeteria. Mom is behind the wheel of her golden Dodge Minivan, which has days it doesn't want to drive us anywhere, just coughs every time mom tries to start up the engine. Today it's running just fine and mom takes it as a good sign. When you're Polish you're into signs and stuff that can tell or alter your fate. Things like: no one ever gets married in May because that would doom your marriage; and you should never start work on a Friday because that's the end of the week and would bring you bad luck; and always tie a red ribbon around a newborn's crib and stroller to chase the bad spirits away.

Today is a Friday, and in the morning I told mom about the bad luck. She was brushing her short hair in the bathroom, all of it flat in the back, and the comb was constantly missing the spot. She watched herself in the mirror, sucking on her lower lip and said: "Yeah, but we are just going to *see* what this job is about, not work, right?" I shrugged and left the room.

Common Boundary

In the car I keep scrubbing off the leftovers of my light green nail polish. Basia is in the passenger seat and constantly turns around to talk to me in the back. She's nineteen, "skinny as a mare," as my mom likes to say, and wearing a too small sunflower dress we got at the thrift store by the house. Even though she's nineteen and I'm only ten, she likes to hang out with me because I remind her of her younger brother who's in Poland. Usually we hang around the park, and she lets me smoke a cigarette or two if I promise never to tell. Most of the time she tells me stories about the boyfriend she left in Poland and other things that I also had to promise not to tell. I mostly listen. Being ten years old usually means not having too many romantic stories to share. Don't want to tell her how I like Andy, who made me touch a dead frog on the side of the road once. My stories are PG-13 at the most, while hers are often rated "R."

"Slow down a bit sexy mama," Basia tells mom who just hit a pothole, making the car rumble and us bob our bodies, my right fingernail sliding off my left one.

She's doing 35 mph in a 20 mph zone even though she doesn't have an Illinois driver's license, but she has a Polish one and the way she sees it, it's much harder to drive in Poland because of all the trams and ramps and one way streets, so a Polish license is more than enough for the

American roads. The car's air-conditioner is busted, so Basia has her window down, but mom refuses to pull her window down because she believes the wind can make you sick. I can feel the tiny sweat bubbles forming behind my bangs, which I wear thick and long to cover up the pimples. Basia takes her loose, curly hair into her hand and twists it into a bun, then lets it loose again.

"So how can I ask him: 'What is the pay?'" She smiles, and my mom laughs softly as she hits another pothole. I think about the answer, but all that comes to mind is the phrase, "How much money?" – which sounds kind of wrong, but that's all I got. Before I tell them this, mom starts panicking about her English.

"How can I understand the kids? What can they ask me?"

"They can say, 'I want pizza,' and then you give them a slice of pizza," I say from the back, and Basia smiles at me, the way she usually does when mom freaks out about something.

"'I want pizza?'" mom repeats.

"Or you can just ask, 'This?' if you are not sure and they'll nod."

"I don't know, this seems difficult," mom says looking for reassurance; I watch a yellow school bus drive by and think about how it's going to be when I will have to ride in one.

"Not really mom," I say, still fixed on the bus.

She pulls over and a middle-aged guy, kind of short, bald and round, runs up to the car, like he's afraid we'll change our minds and take off or something. Basia instantly opens the door, gets up, and sits in the back. So the guy takes the passenger seat. He smiles at us and shakes hands with each of us, even me. He starts talking, and he's a fast talker. It's hard to separate the words. But sometimes he pauses and seems to wait for an answer, and then everyone waits for me to say something; but sometimes I just stare, so the man repeats some words again, only slowly.

He asks us if we're Polish (like he doesn't know already), and then starts to say all the little words he'd learned, like: "daj mi buzi," "dziendobry," and "paczki," only he mispronounces them all, and it takes me awhile before I even realize that he's speaking in Polish. He has this wide grin on his face, and my mom is repeating all the words after him, only in the way they should be pronounced, and the guy laughs and we echo his laughter, although I don't think any of this is really funny.

Then he is searching through some papers, like a business person, and takes out one sheet, waving it at my mom, who's doing 45 in a 30 mph zone, and I know that even when she would be able to take the paper and read it top to bottom, she wouldn't have a clue about what it says. So the guy shows this paper to Basia, who then passes it to me, and it's like a form or something, with blank lines and prices.

"It's a uniform order form. I must complete it because you need to have uniforms in order to work in the school," he says, looking at me looking at the paper. "It costs usually around ninety dollars per one uniform, so it's a hundred and eighty for two, and you must order at least one or two per person," he says slowly, raising his bushy eyebrows. Then Basia is looking at me and mom is not saying anything, but I know they are both waiting for me to translate, and I know they both heard the 'dollar' word because everyone is tense and not moving at all, just waiting for me to speak.

"He says you need to pay him hundred and eighty dollars for the 'uniforms' for the job." My mom, the sun in her eyes, loses her smile and gets this awkward look on her face. She tries to hide it with her make-up and expensive perfume that she wears on special occasions when she tries to appear classy, but still, I can tell she's thinking hard about the money.

"Hundred and eighty," mom repeats, and the man starts saying things about American schools and all this other stuff no one listens to or understands because I know my mom is trying to calculate in her head how long it takes her to save that amount of money; and Basia is staring at the back of my mother's head, wishing she could have some alone time with mom to talk things over, but the stranger is here and we're already on the way to the school, and we don't want to be wasting anyone's time. So mom finally says: "Okay," but says it flatly, no smile. The man nods and says he needs to know their sizes for the uniforms. He asks mom if she's a small, and mom lights up at this and says: "Small, small – no, M size," and the man keeps on telling her: "You look like a small," and mom keeps on turning her head "no," but laughing at the same time, while the sun slowly moves out of her face.

After he took their money and showed us around the school and the cafeteria, he promised to call in two weeks, "When the real school starts." We waited three weeks and kept on calling, but his machine always gave us the beep. Then we went back to the school to look for him. They didn't see him for awhile; he was really a janitor and the person who talked to us seemed shocked that we paid him money. They didn't need any cafeteria workers. So mom and Basia turned around and went down the dark hallway to the front door. Mom was wearing polyester sweat pants, and they kept on rustling every time she moved.

We could hear the words: "Good Luck," fly behind us, but no one looked at me, so I didn't say anything; no one said anything all the way back.

◊ ~◆~ ◊

". . . the world is a country which nobody ever yet knew by
description: one must travel through it one's self to be
acquainted with it."

-    Lord Chesterfield

"In every country its own custom."

-    Old Proverb

◊ ~◆~ ◊

Beginning in the Midwest

Rewa Zeinati

I slept on the futon in the living room the first time my husband was on night-call. I couldn't bring myself to sleep in the bedroom. It felt so isolated and far from the apartment door, which was reasonably the closest thing to my husband without actually having to go to the hospital, where he was obviously within reach. Of course there was no sleeping involved; I just kept tossing and turning, unable to focus on anything but the literal and metaphorical darkness I found myself in. It was the first time I've slept completely alone in a new place in a country thousands of miles away from what I used to call my only home. I had no friends, and I was not familiar with Saint Louis, but of course I've known about the U.S. and I've watched American movies back in Beirut. (Speaking of American movies, I always wanted to eat takeaway Chinese food out of the tiny white box as they do, and that was one of the first things I did when I moved here.) The truth is, my life in Saint Louis began during my third year in the United States; the first two years were spent in Iowa

City, during which my husband was a Research Fellow, so he was able to sleep at home every night. But when we moved to Saint Louis, it might as well have been my first year away.

I was twenty-three when I got married to my husband, who was only beginning his future as a fresh graduate from medical school. My mother warned me about moving so far to a place where I had never lived and knew no one, and she asked me repeatedly about my decision, that regardless of my love, did I really understand what I was getting myself into, marrying a doctor who is still in training? Generally it was every Middle Eastern parent's dream that her daughter get married to a doctor and that her son become either a doctor, lawyer or engineer, but still my mother, ever the practical one, worried about the fact that he was going to be busy often, and I might find it too hard to be alone for long days and sometimes nights at a time.

Iowa City had its own set of culture shocks. I had no idea what people meant when they asked me, "So how are you dealing with the culture shock of moving to the USA?" considering we were in Iowa City, which was not quite a city in my eyes. Did they mean it was too busy, too modern, too Western, compared to the third world country I came from? Or did they in fact imply that I came from the renowned bustling Beirut to a quiet Midwestern town where the population did not much exceed 60,000 people, and mustn't I be bored by loneliness? I never asked, but I soon realized that most people here didn't travel much out of state, and moving away was usually a single flight away from home, compared to the 24 hour ordeal across oceans and land, once a year, if not years at a time.

But the West was, and continues to be, everywhere; we are already familiar with it, without even living there. It's even taken over our morning coffee. Starbucks is big in Lebanon, in Beirut mainly. Even though the prices are criminal, people come by in swarms to buy a Tall decaffeinated, skinny latte or something Venti, imagining they are experiencing that age-old romantic notion of the West being the land of opportunity where dreams happen. And that, in a way, is the truth.

I didn't know what to expect when the plane landed in Iowa City. I came through Minneapolis, Saint Paul, where I was already confused that the airport had more than one name, and was worried I was going to get lost or miss my flight or suddenly forget the whole English language. I held the chest x-ray I was required to take before coming here (in my hand as if my life depended on it) all the way from Beirut to Iowa City, not sure who was going to ask me for it at any moment during the trip. I was of course "randomly" selected every single time upon my arrival, was taken into a private room where I was searched considerably, was asked several times if I had in fact packed the bags that I had with me, and that in fact I knew exactly what was in each, and that no one was in the room with me when I packed. Of course there was someone in the room with me when I packed my bags! I was alone when I came here, but back there moving away is an insanely public experience. I didn't need to mention that, of course. I just nodded all the way through and said yes whenever I had to. I also smiled a lot, anything to keep me from falling apart. My future was beginning right before my eyes, and I missed my family immediately and my husband all at once, since I had to wait two months before I followed him, due to the endless amount of paperwork I needed to deal with before traveling, to gain permission for entry.

Throughout the first two years I kept myself busy. My husband went to work, and I stayed home and discovered what the whole fuss was about when it came to cooking. I cleaned our tiny apartment, which didn't take long at all, and did our laundry, things I never had to deal with before. I walked in the streets, learned how to use the bus system, and emailed home, long emails from my husband's computer at work (we didn't own one yet) that took time to write and even longer to send because I didn't want loved ones to worry that I was sad; but at the same time I missed them terribly, and so

I felt the need to choose my words carefully. Moreover, I had all the time in the world on my hands.

For the first time I was able to see Lebanon from a distance, and I longed for it like I've never longed for anything in my life. I watched CNN and Fox News, and it was during that time that the invasion of Iraq was about to take place; I quickly found myself becoming infuriated at the media and the lies we were made to believe as truths and justification for war. I was never interested in politics before I moved to the United States, and the more I read and heard, the more I wanted to know, and the more I felt it was my duty to alter the false realities that surrounded me. I wrote opinion letters about the war to local newspapers, and at every chance I let people know that those across the Atlantic who speak Arabic and who pray to Allah were my friends, that they are in fact people who are praying to the same god that's found here in the United States of America. "Shock and awe" were among some of the responses.

On the other hand, I appreciated the warmth of the American people; everyone said hello and good morning and good evening, even while merely passing me by on the streets, and I was comforted by these pleasant faces and affectionate demeanors. While longing for the chaos I was familiar with, I was comforted by the fact that everything was organized and clean, signs were everywhere, and it was difficult to get lost even if I wanted to. At the same time, I had some reservations. I hunted for jobs with an undergraduate degree in English Literature, from a foreign university of course, and it was here that I began to question my major. All of a sudden, English seemed to be the language of imperialism and propaganda, and I was angry at myself for becoming a part of it so early on, without realizing it, and even angrier that I had to take things so personally as well. I decided to make the best of it and turn it all around in favorable ways; I eventually earned a Masters in Creative Writing and started up my passion for painting, realizing there are other ways I can speak out and give myself a voice that can be heard in constructive ways, as a woman and as a foreigner. But the more I read the news the more I felt let down. I realized how language became obsolete and meaning twisted in the most treacherous ways. Unfortunately, those who owned the language owned the "truth."

Finding a job in Iowa City was challenging, if not exasperating, and I ended up working part time as a bookseller in a Barnes & Noble store because that was the only place that would take me, but it was not quite the place where I wanted to start a career. Of course being surrounded by books for hours at a time gave me no reason for complaint. And so time passed, two strong winters and far too many choices at the supermarket, all but the kind of pita bread that I couldn't find anywhere and missed like a lost limb. I was too excited to experience new things that I did not foresee the level of yearning that I would feel for home and for everything that represented and reminded me of it. Like anything that is loved from a distance, there's the risk of falling into the false perception that elsewhere is where perfection lies, but I have to admit that not only did I see the beauty that I took for granted back home, but I also recognized the falsehood and corruption that were breeding there as well, and then I remembered the reasons why I was away in the first place. There were times I couldn't bear the homesickness, and the mellowness of Iowa City didn't help in keeping me distracted. But two years later we moved to Saint Louis for my husband's career. Still the Midwest, still the severe storms that I could never get used to, still an airport that wasn't entirely international, but it felt more like a city to me. I also had the opportunity to visit other cities around the nation.

I didn't come to the United States with ten dollars in my pocket, like a lot of older immigrants, but the difference was that then, the whole family would move away and *become* that new place, spilling children and grandchildren who would only hear stories of their ancestors' original homes. I, on the other hand, came alone, with a lot more than ten bucks in my pocket, to my husband and nothing but the promise of a great future founded on good education and good health. I wonder who had it harder.

When I think about the places where I grew up, I should immediately think of Lebanon and the Arab region because that is where I lived until I was twenty three years young, but the truth is, the United States is where I grew up. Here is where I've grown to love what I took for granted, to appreciate the things that I never thought twice about, like age and health, and the value of love and friendship. Here is where I've learned to count on myself and to enjoy my own company, to discover ways of building the future that I've all too happily picked for myself without anticipating the real consequences of my choices, and I am thankful that I didn't. I visit Lebanon whenever I can, and I continuously miss it even when I'm there, and sometimes especially. I could leave what I used to call home and travel far, but where do I go from the *home* that was born inside me? There is no escaping it, and years later I am a United States citizen in these unfortunately hostile times, a citizen with two identities, and many more to embrace. Must we be one *or* the other? We are nothing if not an anthology of our experiences and the places we've lived and traveled. I find solace in the words of the

Lebanese writer Amin Maalouf, who said in his book *In the Name of Identity: Violence and the Need to Belong*, "What makes me myself rather than anyone else is the very fact that I am poised between two countries, two or three languages, and several cultural traditions. It is precisely this that defines my identity. Would I exist more authentically if I cut off a part of myself?"

◊ ~◆~ ◊

"We think according to nature; we speak according to rules; but we act according to custom."

- Francis Bacon

"Good company in a journey makes the way to seem the shorter."

- Izaak Walton

◊ ~◆~ ◊

Emigrées

Roy Jacobstein

—"Imagine the small empty purse
your mother carried across an ocean."

Only now, in the airport waiting area,
riffling through a discarded *Redbook*
as our century passes its worn baton
to the next, do I vision her exodus

from Pilvestok, detritus of the First
World War. She'd have been three,
maybe four, already the trachoma
clouding her corneas, veiling her

from her own sight, threatening
to snuff the Statue's welcome lamp.

Common Boundary

Did she grasp her Papa's hand the way
he grasped at prayer? And in her other

hand—what? A doll with blue clear eyes?
German fairy tales? Or perhaps a lemon,
its rough skin staining her palm for life,
so each time she touched hand to face

the next eight decades she'd inhale
that bitter scent, hear her sisters retching
again into the shadows of steerage,
and claw deeper into the hard ground.

~

Ceremony

At the end of the blessing
ceremony held for you
at the neighborhood *wat*
on the rutted dirt road
near the Silver Palace,
after the monk had chanted
the sacred Pali texts

in his steady bass monotone

(for what seemed three hours

to my creaking knees)

and sprinkled your head

with jasmine-scent,

he pulled his cell phone

from beneath his saffron robe

and took a call, and we knew

it was time to take you

half the globe home. And now,

when the Doubts arise, fears

for a world of bombs and spores

and mandatory veils, I nuzzle

my long nose along your tan chest

while chanting my own bass tune,

a maneuver that never fails

to elicit a startled laugh,

and your legs pedal the temperate air,

and your anklets chinkle,

and the thin red cord

the monk tied to your left wrist

gleams brighter than any gold,

telling us all goes well, and will,

for you are home.

Passover

Humming, Aunt Bea ladles *knadlach*:
matzo-ball boulders in a yellow sea.
Soon all four Aunts will rise and merge

again in the kitchen—that long unbroken
lineage: shtetl, sister and steam. Pinochle
will claim the uncles, cousins will scatter,

some to swap baseball cards, some to dress
dolls, but I'll return to the photos,
fixed between those little black triangles.

Here's Uncle Herman's bayonet, gleaming
in the Prussian sun. This one is Uncle Saul,
in the shadows of steerage, his goodbyes

to Smyrna already uttered in four tongues.
And over here, on that railroad platform,
the slim teenager singing for the last Tsar—

Nicholas II, who sits so straight between

his uniformed guards on the royal train—

that's Aunt Bea, at the front of the chorus

of village girls spilling out their dark eyes.

~

Beyond the Gauze Curtain

Everyone seems to have one,

in a position of prominence,

as I do over the wooden mantel

of the gas-fueled fireplace,

a grainy black-and-white photograph

in a gilt-edged frame. A grandparent,

or a more distant ancestor—say, great-

great-grandmother Hannah

from the old country, somewhere

beyond the pale, in what today

might be Belarus. Or maybe it's Maudie

from County Clare, the one who later

headed out to Utah with her Swede.

Common Boundary

Or most distant of all, oneself, held aloft
by beaming parents and clutching Bear
with such small hands. Beyond the gauze
curtain, beyond the window, how tall
was the wheat? Where were the wars?
Was it the year cousin Nora eloped
or the year her father died? Everyone
is here before the shutter, as close
as the minute that has just now passed.

Living Between Question Marks

Ruth Knafo Setton

I have come to the heart of the heart of my heart. A new
country. I don't remember this hotel, café, street of blue
torches. I have been in this city a thousand times: I have
never been here. I say words I must have said before, but
they blister my tongue and ache between my teeth until I utter
them, raw and unformed: a new language.

- from The Road to Fez

I dream in French, write in English, mysteriously know
Spanish, curse in Arabic, cry in Hebrew.

I was born in Morocco, spoke French before English, and
didn't learn Hebrew till I was in my twenties, but instantly felt
a profound affinity to languages that move from right to left,
notebooks that move from back to front. I entered my new
country – English – through books, word by word, letter by
delicious letter. At fourteen, I made a decision that seemed
climactic even then: I chose English as the language in which
I'd write. French retreated to shadows in the corners of my

room, memories that felt like wind on my cheeks and that smelled like the sea.

But in the beginning, French was music – a song punctuated by hushed Arabic – the language my parents refused to teach us, the children, and kept as their secret language. They told jokes in French, intricate, elaborate stories embellished with myths, legends and historical facts that built to a final punch line always delivered in pungent, concise Arabic. When we kids begged for a translation, they'd say, "Sorry, it can't be done." I'm sure that affected me: growing up hearing amazing jokes, stories and narratives, and not getting the last line, the final wry twist that brings it all together. In that sense it was a very postmodern childhood, straining to grasp stories that emerged in fragments, whispers, gestures and facial expressions – tongues clicking, eyebrows raised. And the final realization that the ending is a promise that isn't always fulfilled.

It makes sense that I exist between languages, roam between countries, write between genres – poetry, fiction and nonfiction – and that, in a sense, I'm always writing in translation. Growing up, I heard my parents speak four languages in a single sentence. When I wrote my first novel, *The Road to Fez*, my editor agreed: no italics. After all, which language was the foreign language?

It took me a while to understand that my parents' groping toward English, and mine toward a complete identity, the crazy jokes and fractured tales of a life in North Africa, were all songs of exile and yearning. Songs of diaspora. Songs of the between.

I'm about three in the last photo taken of me before my parents and I leave Morocco for the United States. Curly blonde hair pulled back in a ponytail. Tiny white dress, sturdy bare legs. Light eyes that look questioningly at the photographer, or at the street ahead of me. A small wanderer through life, I clutch a black purse and pause, only for an instant, on my journey. I am resolute, firmly rooted, feet in black patent leather shoes gripping the tiled outdoor corridor. My lips are dark, as if I've just eaten a plum and traces of the juice have stained my lips. Unsmiling, confident that in a moment I will continue on my path to the future, I can afford to let the photographer freeze me. What he doesn't know, what I don't yet know, is that in another moment, my patent leather shoes will be lifted from the tiles, will dangle in the air as I hover between two worlds – the New and the Old, belonging to neither, clinging to both.

What happened to that girl? Did she live a parallel life to mine in the dim, powerful Morocco of my memory? Did she study? Was she married off early, as soon as her blood came?

Was she afraid of the Arabs? Mistreated for being a Jew? Did she fall in love with a boy at school? Sneak out to meet him at the *souk*? Did she walk along the sea with him? I want that girl, I want to smell her flesh, to kiss the back of her knee, to see if her ears are dainty whorled seashells like mine, her eyes as wide, her hands as yearning. What became of her? I feel the pain of exile. I was ripped from her. The girl who crossed the ocean is already the shadow of myself. Right now when you think I am looking at you, I'm looking for her – across the mountains and seas – wondering if she even knows I exist, if she misses me at all.

Sometimes I think I've been writing *her* story all along, the girl I might have been, the girl who could have been me.

~

My grandfather is my first memory: he twines a flower around my ear. A border-crosser, he was a poet who wrote in classical Arabic, a musician who played the oud at both Arab and Jewish events, a man who took over the rooftop, traditionally the woman's space, and created his own refuge there with books, flowers and two enormous brass cages where he kept fifty homing pigeons. I picture him on that roof, refusing to lock the cages of his pigeons, painting their wings to create beauty in a dark world, attaching messages and prayers to their legs and watching them fly off to places he, as a Jew, could not go to. Oddly – or maybe not so oddly – the pigeons always returned to him.

On the wall of my grandparents' house hung a brass key to their old house. My grandfather described the house in intimate loving detail: birds singing in the blue courtyard, sparkling fountains, orange tree . . . .

It wasn't until much later that I learned that the house my grandfather described was the house in Toledo, Spain the family had fled during the Inquisition!

Time passes differently in the East. It circles and bites its own tail. It stands still for hours, then leaps into the future, and somersaults into the past. As Godard says, "Every story has a beginning, middle and end, but not necessarily in that order."

In a Sephardic legend, a family returns to the house in Spain after 500 years away, turns the key in the lock, and the door opens. After my grandfather's death, the brass key disappeared. Someone later claimed it had never been on the wall, and that I'd imagined it.

~

Punctuation is a matter of grave importance to me, as a writer of course, but also as someone whose life is a hyphen. It shouldn't be surprising that my favorite punctuation mark is the dash, that I do my breathing, thinking, writing, living between the certainties. Not the period. So arrogant, so final. Not: this is it. Not: this OR this. But this AND this. AND this too. AND throw that in as well. For me there's always more, always another way of looking at life, another window or door, another perspective. My writing, like much Sephardic writing, is composed of multiple points of view, fragments, dislocated narratives linked by dashes.

And from the first moment I saw the Spanish question marks – one inverted and one right side up – that bracket questions, I shivered with pleasure. I thought, I can live between these question marks. There is something very Jewish about Spanish question marks. Maybe something female too. They question the very essence of the question and make concrete what is implicit: that the inner mystery is contained, almost protected, within the two question marks. Like the Moroccan courtyard, in which the truth is turned inward. Like my grandfather living between two worlds – the historical reality of Spain and the imagined reality of the future in Jerusalem – while standing on his rooftop.

~

We are Jews with a Mediterranean accent who carry the memory of the sun in our hearts. Enter our houses in the mellah or juderia and go directly to the soul – the tiled inner courtyard crowded with women and children – like us, hidden, secretive, restless. Dance with us: flamenco guitar and hypnotic desert oud, drums that pound like bare feet running on a beach, nostalgic and mournful yet always with a beat that circles on itself. Look at our family photos: men wearing tasseled fezzes and djellabahs, women with painted icon faces and pointed babouches beneath silver-threaded caftans. Eat with us: bstilla, with its exquisite commingling of sweet and savory, fragrant couscous, salads vivid with color and wit, and flaky orange-scented desserts that tingle your senses with their beauty and then melt on your tongue. After the meal join us in the salon arabe for mint tea or cardamom-spiced coffee, and discuss the destiny of the Jews, the concept of home and identity, and tell Johra stories in Arabic, French, Hebrew, Spanish and English – all in the same sentence. Laugh until you cry. Remember the sun.

~

I'll close with a recipe, which is fitting since Moroccan Jews translate almost everything into food.

RUTH'S IMMIGRANT STEW

In a large pot, stir misconceptions, superstitions, dreams, fears, excessive closeness.

Throw in a handful of fresh wild mint your grandfather grew on the rooftop . . . the carrots and broccoli your mother swore would sprout from your scalp if you didn't shampoo your hair . . . sardines freshly caught in the net and grilled in olive oil at the port . . . the stone your father used to set on the seat of a bus leaving his hometown, Safi, and pretend it was him traveling away . . . .

Add a pinch of exile, that spice that ensures that no food will ever taste as good as your grandmother's, no sunset appear as beautiful as the one back there, no house as homelike as the one you left behind.

Season with cumin, garlic, onion, turmeric. Rub fresh kzboor between your palms & scatter.

Stir with a brass key.

While you breathe in the aromas, listen to your mother explain the art of cooking: Don't be obvious. Mix the unexpected: chicken, eggs and almonds baked in phyllo dough and sprinkled with confectioner's sugar; jam made from sweet baby eggplants and walnuts; tagines simmering with saffron and za'atar. And my daughter, never forget the importance of cinnamon.

And your father's words: you can go anywhere, be anything – but stay invisible.

And your grandfather telling you before he died: You are my roots. You and your children will plant the seeds of my memory in your words.

Stir until the stew boils and froths out of the pot. Write the recipe in four languages, leaving out one crucial ingredient (because you're used to doing it in your head, not on paper).

Serve with complaints and self-deprecation: if you had tasted this in the old days, when I had the right herbs and the eggplants were the tiny purple ones, not these huge hulking ones with no taste, and of course, the couscous was pounded by hand and steamed in a couscousier . . . .

Before your guests have finished eating, insist they take seconds. Hover over them like a human question mark. Reach toward them like a dash—

~

My Father Eats Figs

My father eats figs
the way he eats his past,
spits out the skin.

He eats figs and stares
out the window at Mrs. Grimm's
curtains: she knows

our secret, how we emerged
from the jungle. She watches me
with green eyes and razor lips.

Witch, djinn, she eats children
and buries their bones
in her backyard—I've been there.

My father eats figs
the way he and his father
ate eggs on the farm

of the other world:
boiled in their shells—
peeled and swallowed

whole, devouring a hundred
at a time. He eats figs, watches
my sister and me, white tulle

and ballet shoes, arms raised,
as we pirouette
on broken pavement.

Mom mans the record player.
Neighbors watch.
Dancing dolls with painted

cheeks, swaying like the palms
we've already forgotten.
The phone rings—Dad runs inside.

We dance and dance,
and it's years
before we see him again.

◊ ～◆～ ◊

"Never can custom conquer nature; for she is ever
unconquered."

-    Cicero

"The country, companions, and the length of your journey
will afford a hundred compensations for your toil."

-    Ovid

◊ ～◆～ ◊

Fig

Eva Konstantopoulos

Fig\, n. [F. figue the fruit of the tree, Pr. figa, fr. L. ficus fig tree, fig. Cf. Fico.]

1. (Bot.) a small fruit tree (Ficus Carica) with large leaves, known from the remotest antiquity. It was probably native from Syria westward to the Canary Islands: We spent all morning climbing down the valley, over rocks and shrubs, to find the fig tree where my father fell from as a child. **2.** The fruit of a fig tree, which is of round or oblong shape, and of various colors: We pulled the fruit from the branches; the honey was dripping from the plump bottom, a drop of dew. Tearing open the green flesh, we raked our tongues through the ripe, red insides. The seeds clung to our fingers, making our hands sticky. **3.** Any of various plants having a fruit somewhat resembling this: You are Greek, not Italian, not Mexican, not Moroccan. You are what I say you are. You are white. You are nothing. You are what I see. **4.** A small piece of tobacco. [U.S.] I didn't want to smoke it, but I did my best when you placed the stick between my fingers. I watched you and then went behind the pool house and sat on a rock. I tried to mimic how you breathed, pulling the smoke in and out of your lungs, again and again. **5.** The value of a fig, practically nothing; a fico; – used in scorn or contempt: Your help wasn't worth a fig. That's what you said, and I laughed at you. I couldn't help it. Don't you see? I was doing my best. The sun was hot and sweat was baked on our skin, white rivulets of salt trailing down our arms. We were building the pool to look like our neighbors', but they had twenty construction workers, and we only had us. **6.** Dress; in full fig: I pulled my shirt over my head, took off the skirt you had been fingering all night. Then I stood in your living room and waited for you to touch me, but you didn't come any closer. I held my breath, closed my eyes. Hoped I'd feel you soon. **7.** Physical condition; shape: I kept eating them, one after the other. Filling the rest in the plastic bucket Thea had given me. She said, "Child, you're going to turn into a fig!" I liked the idea, so I scraped my teeth down the ready insides, the seeds awash in my mouth like tiny needles – oblong bodies – swimming.

~

Also, See: **A.** Fig dust, a preparation of fine oatmeal for feeding caged birds: The first day my father came to New York, he reached for a fig in the flowered bowl. Yota slapped his hand away. "Did you forget? My children eat before you!" **B.** Fig faun, one of a class of rural deities or monsters supposed to live on figs. "Therefore shall dragons dwell there with the fig fauns." – Jer. i. 39. (Douay version): The bee came out of the tree, perched on the fleshy part of my baby arm. When it stung me, I cried 'till dusk, my little face blotchy and squished up like a lemon. Theo couldn't bear it. That night, he went into the shed and brought out some kerosene. Poured the liquid on the trunk and over the big, faun leaves. Then he lit a match. The bees rose – furious, yelling. They soared over our heads, circling the blaze, and then flew up to the stars, the night sky. "No more bad spirits," he told Thea. "No more." *Or:* We weren't allowed to leave the village at Noon. The sun was too high – bending the air around us. Yiayia said the devil would surely find us. It had happened before. **C.** Fig gnat (Zo["o]l.), a small fly said to be injurious to figs: After my father turned fifteen, the fig trees around Yiayia's house stopped bearing fruit. They said it had something to do with the soil, but I think it was the fire ants. Mean little creatures herding over the branches, journeying to the green, budding tips, and those flies – buzzing around the top as if they were things long dead. **D.** Fig leaf, the leaf tree; hence, in allusion to the first clothing of Adam and Eve (Genesis iii.7), a covering for a thing that ought to be concealed; a symbol for affected modesty: In the village, no one used the church, except for Easter. They had to lock it up the rest of the months for fear that the thieves would return – they had already looted the golden relics, the paintings of men with their eyes tilted to the sky. **E.** Fig marigold (Bot.), the name of several plants of the genus Mesembryanthemum, some of which are prized for the brilliancy and beauty of their flowers: "You have a light inside of you . . ." he said. "That is if you don't get pregnant." We were related. He was watching my sister and me draw chalk cats and men on the driveway. He squinted away from us, the smell of wood and meat billowing up from the grill, and my dad, poking the coals with a skewer, the flames dancing, dancing in the afternoon light. **F.** Fig tree (Bot.), any tree of the genus Ficus, but especially F. Carica which produces the fig of commerce: I went to the village and the old women spit on the ground for me, and the old men circled me arms raised. My cousin set me straight. "You're nothing, you know that? Who you are, you come from nothing, so that means you are nothing, too." I agreed with him. I had to. Thousands of miles from home, it was all that I could do.

What We Call Home

Nahid Rachlin

Even after a week, Mohtaram could not believe that her sister, Narghes, was really with her in the living room of her house. But there she was, her polka dot *chador* wrapped around her, sitting in a patch of the sun on the rug in the living room to warm her legs, although it was late May and the temperature hovered around seventy. The house too had marks of Narghes' presence – the presents she had brought: a cloth with paisley designs covered the kitchen table, a tapestry depicting a caravan hung on a wall. The smell of rose water that Narghes dabbed on her clothes permeated the air.

It made Mohtaram feel more at home in her own house since her sister had come. She had not really known what she was getting herself into when she had sold everything she had in Iran, after her husband died, and came to America to live near her son, how much she would be leaving behind; so much would be out of her reach. She had not even known that her son she had come to be near would not be that accessible to her. She saw Cyrus only a few moments every day when he stopped in before he went to the university in Athens to do his teaching. When his children were younger she saw them every day, but now they were at school and busy with their friends. Mildred, Cyrus' wife, had not learned Farsi, and her own English was not all that good so they could not really talk to each other. Feri, her daughter, who had come to America shortly after Cyrus, was studying in Madison and was married to an Iranian engineer, but Mohtaram rarely saw her. She had a few Iranian friends who lived in town, but they were all younger than she, with different concerns.

Before Narghes came, Mohtaram had spent days preparing for the visit – dusting every corner, washing the bedspreads, curtains, tablecloths, scrubbing pots and pans, buying a side of mutton from the young man who slaughtered a sheep every few weeks in the Muslim fashion and sold it to other Iranians in town. For years she had been asking Narghes to come for a visit. She wrote to her. "You will love Ohio. It is sparkling clean with no dust to settle on things. There are many trees and lakes and rivers . . ." Narghes had always refused, saying, "I have my prayer sessions starting next month," or "Bahman wants to get married and we're looking for a proper wife for him." What had prompted her to come now, Narghes had told her, was a dream she had. In the dream she was searching for Mohtaram and finally found her in a wide, well-lit but empty street, scratched and bleeding. The dream had so shaken her that she decided she must see her sister immediately.

In a few moments Mohtaram took Narghes to the shopping center, which was within walking distance, to buy shoes for her. She had been complaining that her feet hurt. Already, in one week, Mohtaram was falling into the old interdependency with her sister. Every day they woke at dawn, prayed, cooked and ate together, and went out for walks. Narghes put on her *chador*, Mohtaram a long-sleeved dress and a scarf on her head. Although Narghes complained about her feet and walked rather slowly, she gave the impression of being the stronger of the two with sturdy arms and ample breasts. Mohtaram felt thin and frail by contrast and was aware that her fairer skin had wrinkled more. It was hard to tell, she was sure, which one of them was older, even though there was a five-year difference in age between them. People occasionally turned around and looked at Narghes in her long black *chador*, and some smiled at her, but just as often they acted as if they did not notice anything different.

"See, they leave you alone here," Mohtaram said. "No one interferes in your affairs."

"But it's so lonely, it's like everyone has crawled into a shell," Narghes said.

Common Boundary

It seemed to Mohtaram that it would have been more natural to Narghes if people stared or even poked at her *chador* and asked her what it was.

One thing, though, caught Narghes' attention, which she liked – a pair of soft, flat shoes in the window of a dime store. "They look so comfortable. They'll be perfect for me," she said. "I constantly change shoes and never find any that fit."

They went in and Narghes tried on the shoes. They were imported from Japan and cost only five dollars. She bought two pairs and wore one pair on the way back. She said they felt as comfortable as they looked.

When they got back, they began to prepare lunch. Today, Feri and Sohrab were driving in from Madison to spend the weekend in Athens, planning to stay with Cyrus and visiting here during the day. They were all coming to the house for lunch soon. Mohtaram had also invited an Iranian couple living nearby to come for lunch. Narghes helped her – cutting eggplants, green beans, cucumbers, soaking the rice, raisins and lentils. They used some of the spices Narghes had brought with her – tumeric, sumac, dried ground lemon, a combination of coriander, cinnamon and pepper. The air was filled with scents Mohtaram associated with home. As they prepared, Narghes filled in Mohtaram with other stories, about the relatives, the brothers, nephews, nieces and aunts and uncles all living in houses near each other in a network of alleys off Ghanat Abad Avenue.

Mohtaram, though, thought with all the detailed accounts there was something imprecise and foggy about her sister's descriptions of people. She wished she could see them herself.

~

Cyrus arrived first. He came into the living room and said, "Mildred had a cold and couldn't come, but she sent this." He held out a large platter. "Apple pie, especially for you, Aunt Narghes."

"You all have been so kind to me," Narghes said. "It makes me . . . ashamed."

Cyrus walked into the kitchen and put the pie on the counter. He took out packs of beer from a bag he was holding and put them in the refrigerator. He was only sixteen years younger than his mother and had alert brown eyes, curly hair and muscular arms from lifting weights every day, one habit he had kept from his adolescent years in Iran, Mohtaram had noticed. He came back into the living room and sat on the semi-circular sofa.

Narghes gathered her legs under her. "I ache all the time. I'm on the way to my grave."

"Don't say such things," Cyrus said. "People here get

married at your age and start a new life."

Mohtaram took the potatoes she had sliced into the kitchen to fry them, but she kept her eyes half way on Narghes and Cyrus. She wanted to make sure no misunderstanding would develop between them, as when, in a previous visit, Narghes had told him bluntly that unless he had had a Muslim wedding ceremony his marriage to Mildred was not valid; Cyrus had flushed and had not answered. Mohtaram had explained for him, "I made sure to marry them with the Koran myself. I said the words and they both went along with it. I converted her first into Islam and gave her the name Zobeideh."

"Tell me all about Uncle Mohammed and Uncle Ahmad," Cyrus was saying to Narghes. "I haven't had any news from them for years."

"What is there to say about them?" But she went on to talk about her brothers at length. Uncle Mohammed had retired from his job as a clerk in the City Hall and spent his days going to the mosque or on pilgrimages with his wife. Uncle Ahmad had a gall bladder removed. There were some noises outside of the house, a car pulling in, and then footsteps.

"It must be them, Feri and Sohrab," Mohtaram said from the kitchen and went to open the outside door. "Come in, come in." She kissed Feri and Sohrab, and they all went inside. Feri dashed to her aunt and they embraced and kissed. Then she introduced her and Sohrab to each other.

"You are still as pretty as ever," Narghes said to her.

"Thank you. I've been counting the days to see you. I had final exams, or else I would have been here much sooner," Feri said.

Then they all sat down. In a few moments Narghes took out from her purse two matching gold pendants with "Allah" inscribed on them in Arabic script and gave one to Sohrab and the other to Feri. Feri and Sohrab thanked her and put them on. Mohtaram thought the pendants looked a little strange on them with their short haircuts, blue jeans, and wild looking tee shirts. Sohrab engaged Cyrus in conversation while Narghes and Feri talked between themselves.

"Have you thought of children yet? You're almost thirty; time is running out for you," Narghes said to Feri.

"I've been too busy to think about it," Feri said.

"You don't want to end up childless like me."

"Yes, Aunt Narghes, tell her that," Sohrab said, turning to them.

Feri laughed and leaned against his chest. He stroked her cheeks for a moment and then let go.

"Let's play some records," Cyrus said. "Persian music for

the occasion. Do you mind, Aunt Narghes?"

Narghes looked into space and nodded her head ambiguously.

He searched through the small stack of records next to the phonograph and put one on. A soft, nasal female voice began to sing, "Oh, my love, you're like a wild flower on the hills, out of my reach, out of my reach."

Mohtaram and Narghes went back and forth into the kitchen, carrying things. They spread a cloth, with hand-blocked designs of camels and trees, on the living room floor and then they set the dishes and silverware on it.

Feri said, "This is interesting, an all-Iranian lunch."

Some footsteps sounded in the driveway again. "Here they are, Mehdi and Simin," Mohtaram said.

Momentarily Mehdi and Simin came in. They glanced around the room, greeting everyone. Mehdi was holding a basket with two chickens, their legs tied with strings. The chickens lay placidly in the basket.

"I brought these so that we can slaughter them the Muslim way for Narghes *khanoom*."

"Thank you, please put them on the porch," Mohtaram said. "We already have a lot to eat today."

"You can save them for later."

"May God pay you back for all your troubles," Narghes

said. "I can't thank you enough."

Mehdi went out through the screen door and laid the chickens on the porch. The chickens began to cluck frantically as if they knew they had little time left to live.

Mohtaram and Narghes brought over the food and put it on the cloth – two stews, two kinds of rice, a yogurt and cucumber salad, *sharbat* to drink, halva and the huge apple pie Cyrus had brought over for dessert.

"Let's sit down and eat," Mohtaram said.

They sat around the cloth and started to eat. Then the pie was served. Narghes refused. Mohtaram said, "Mildred is scrupulous. She must have rinsed everything several times." Narghes still looked hesitant.

"It's just flour, sugar and apples," Mohtaram said, knowing what her sister was worried about. The first night she had arrived, Narghes had inspected everything in the house to make sure it adhered to the Muslim laws. She asked her to read the ingredients in packaged items – crackers, cookies, bread – before she ate them. She had explained to Mohtaram that a young man in their neighborhood in Teheran had told her that they used pork fat when cooking in America.

Narghes took a slice and began to eat it. "It's very good. May God give strength to your wife," she said to Cyrus.

Cyrus smiled. "I'm glad you like it."

After lunch the men sat in one corner and started to drink beer and talk while the women had tea. Feri and Simin went into the kitchen to do the dishes. They were talking rapidly and intensely to each other, their voices occasionally rising above those of the men in the living room. Mehdi was bragging about how much he won every time he went to the horse races, one hundred dollars last time. Sohrab talked about his engineering firm, how the salesmen always went after girls when they traveled, and, he added in a whisper, some call girls were arranged for them by the customers' companies. Then Mehdi said to Cyrus, "You college teachers have all those young girls available to you. They want to be in your favor and so . . ."

Mohtaram was thinking how much closer she felt to her sister than to her children. She observed how aloof her children were by contrast to Narghes. There was something off-hand about them, even when they were trying to be nice. Their attitude toward the occasion, it seemed to her, was that of amusement. When children, they had been like all other Iranian children, dependent on her approval, thriving on her warmth, her cuddling and kissing them, but they had changed. They were cool and independent and egocentric as she imagined most Americans to be. Maybe I have changed also, becoming a little like them. This knowledge hit her for the first time, really upsetting her. Then she thought maybe it is Narghes that makes me feel this way. I must be seeing things through her eyes, for this is how Narghes must be viewing my Americanized children as she sits there looking on quietly.

"There is this student in one of my classes," Cyrus was saying. "She always sits in the first row, crossing her legs and . . ." He paused and then added something that Mohtaram, even though she strained, could not hear. Then all the men began to giggle about something, a private joke maybe.

After a moment Mehdi said, "They don't think of that as being loose morally. I used to think every time a girl smiled at me she meant something by it, but that isn't necessarily the case."

The other two laughed again.

"American girls think nothing of such matters," Cyrus said. "And why should they?"

Mohtaram was aware of Narghes shifting tensely in her place. Just then Narghes broke her silence, but with an unexpected remark. "Mohtaram, why did you do this to me, making me eat the unclean food." Her face went white, her dark eyes rolled upward as if she were delirious.

"Oh, sister, what's wrong?" Mohtaram asked.

"I heard what they were saying in the kitchen."

"What did you hear?"

"The pie Cyrus brought over had been cooked in pig's fat."

"Who said that?"

"Feri said it."

"Feri, come over here," Mohtaram called urgently.

Feri came to the doorway of the room.

"Did you say that the pie crust was cooked in pig's fat?"

"No."

"What did you say then?"

"I was talking about a pie I took to a picnic. I used bacon and ham in it. It was a quiche Lorraine, a French dish."

Simin came into the doorway also. "Yes, Narghes *khanoom*, that's what Feri was telling me."

"Apple pie in pig's fat?" Cyrus said.

"All the sinful talk in this room, and the beer dripping on the rugs where we pray." Narghes looked from face to face. "It was a mistake for me to come to America."

"We just finished the last beer so there won't be any more of it," Cyrus said.

"I'm spoiling the day for you. That's why I shouldn't have come at all. I will return soon," Narghes said.

"If you go back so soon we all will be heart-broken," Feri said.

Narghes lowered her face, in deep contemplation.

Everyone was quiet, enveloped in the tension hanging in the air. Then Cyrus got up and said, "I have to go home, I have a lot of work to get done. And Mildred is left alone." He said goodbye to everyone and left.

"We have to leave also," Mehdi said to Narghes. "But we'll be seeing you again. I'll slaughter the chickens first. I brought along a good knife." He went out through the screen door to the porch. Then he came back and put the chickens, all cleaned up, on the counter. He washed his hands, and he and Simin left. Then Feri and her husband also left to go to Cyrus' house.

"The light is fading. We'd better pray," Narghes said.

"Let me put away the food first," Mohtaram said, going into the kitchen.

Narghes followed. "See how these chickens are lying there, dead and helpless? That's how we will be one day," she said, giving out a sigh. "And imagine if you get ill, who's there to take care of you? You know the dream I had that prompted me to come here. Maybe it meant something. You ought to go back to Iran with me. Put up the house for sale. We'll return together. Everyone will be happy to have you back. You could buy another house there or if you want the two of us will live together in my house."

Mohtaram could see clearly now how lonely and hollow her days had been before Narghes came. She began to cry, tears just trickling down her face as if a dam had broken. "My life has been empty without realizing it," she said. "If I had any sense I would go back with you."

Soon the two of them knelt together, *chadors* on their heads, facing the East, reclining and touching their heads on the *mohr* they put on the floor.

Mohtaram had a hard time concentrating on her prayers. Her mind kept wandering to her childhood – she and Narghes sitting together in the hollowed-out trunk of a sycamore tree in their courtyard, going to the bazaar running parallel to their street, sleeping on the flat roof of their house, talking, looking at the shapes the clouds made, the lit kites circling in the sky, the bright stars. As a child she had been the more gregarious. She recalled Narghes withdrawing into a secluded corner of the courtyard and playing alone with her dolls, saying endearing things to them, picking them up and kissing or spanking them, but Mohtaram would intrude and insist on being included.

Narghes had been haughty and very pretty with greenish-hazel eyes and wavy brown hair, striking against her olive skin. Mohtaram was shorter with smaller bones and less striking features. When the time came, Narghes married a jeweler and made the best of her marriage. She herself married a distant cousin, an accountant she had always had a crush on, and they were happy together. He was hard working and intelligent, the only educated person among a family of merchants. He was healthy and energetic, hard to believe he would die young, from a stroke. Mohtaram still could recall vividly that morning waking up and finding him staring with unmoving eyes into space. She touched him and he was ice cold and rubbery. She screamed and ran out to Narghes' house, a few doors down on the same alley. Narghes had kept her there for days, trying to comfort her . . .

~

That night Mohtaram lay in bed awake for a long time. Memories hit her again, more strongly and vividly in the dark. She saw Narghes and herself in their house, in the hollow of that tree. Now she recalled how the two of them used to sing together, a rhyme they had made up. "I belong to this tree, to this house, to this street, and will never leave them as long as it is in my power to stay."

She wished she could break out of the prison of this new self, and be reborn again into the old one. She fell asleep, and each time she woke she thought the same thing: Narghes is going to leave soon, and the house will become impersonal, barren without her, one of the many houses on the street and yet quite isolated from them.

Near dawn, when she woke, she thought very clearly, I must return with her. This is my chance.

Pass

M. Neelika Jayawardane

For Miriam "Mazi" Makeba:
who collected passports, never kept her pass

Cape Town is a port city in which the contestations that unleashed the inequalities that accompanied the Enlightenment – and the subsequent modernity from which Europeans benefitted – took place. When the Dutch arrived, they used it as a prison colony, much as the U.S. has used Guantanamo Bay – to remove, maroon, and erase political and religious leaders from the South Asian countries they were trying to take over. The VOC first shipped political prisoners here – princes and Imams, and other men of high standing, brought over with entire entourages of family and followers. But later, slave labour became the solution to the drudgery of everyday life. Allesverloren, Vergelegen, and Meerlust – wine farms, some of which have been around since the 1600s – are dotted with stately mansions and wineries constructed by the slave labourers brought from Malaysia, Ceylon, India, and other islands along the Indonesian archipelago – places to which the VOC sent their militarised ships to monopolise the spice trade.

When modern visitors first land on this port, they may realise that the labour that supports the "first world" portion of this nation – those cleaning their hotel rooms, those clearing the streets of rubbish, those cultivating the vines in breathtakingly beautiful vineyards – are the descendants of the same subjugated peoples who were brought here to labour on the roads, buildings, the kitchens, the vineyards: inscribed on their bodies is South Africa's (and European modernity's) deeply exploitative history.

Things *have* changed here in South Africa, but nothing has moved that much.

In my youth, I'd wanted nothing but leaving – the voluminous otherness that was America was such high pleasure that I forgot to return home for nearly a decade. When I left my rural backwater mining town in Southern Africa for an equally backwater college town in the U.S., I thought I'd never return to my origins. I found a way to make a living under various temporary and unstable guises – including being an under-the-table pastry chef – rather than go back and face a broken country's old songs.

But once I found employment at a university in America, I returned to the Cape whenever I had time off. I lived in a cottage in the de Trafford vineyard, settled into the joint between the Helderberg and Stellenbosch mountain ranges: it had an outdoor shower, veiled by the shadow of bluegum trees; I could hear the bark of baboons when leopards chased them down the mountainside. On the Mont Fleur estate, the vineyard workers saw me running through the clay roads before the sun set in the winter, and before the sun rose in the summer; it was a habit I picked up in America.

The sun only peeked over the granite of the mountaintops at 11am, greeted by the excited twittering of Cape white-eyes. Here, I had a lifetime of knowledge about the specificity of birdcalls and migratory patterns: what I had to train my ear for at different times of the year. I usually experience a night or two of insomnia every month – usually associated with full-moon nights. During this period of my life, the insomnia became a regular occurrence; I would wake up at 3am and listen to the nightjars calling out to each other on moonlit nights: "two-two twirlydoooo!" I listened to the voices of the nightbirds, the howling winter winds rustling through fields of fynbos, the bullets of bluegum pods scattering on the roof.

~

At the end of August every year, I returned to a small town in the U.S.: back to my job as a college professor.

Common Boundary

I woke up at 3am, hearing the burbling water-voices of the nightjars.

I looked up at night to the rural, northern sky above the great wash of Lake Ontario, the arc of stars as brilliant as that of my vineyard sky: the long skirt-train of the Milky Way swept the darkness above. Orion, here, existed the wrong way around; and the Southern Cross, the stars composing the two arms as brilliant as finely cut diamonds, a great and lonely absence.

In this northern place I returned to in order to make money, and to have stability, I felt nothing but absence. I was out of place without love to locate my body.

It was here in America that I understood: love is homesickness.

~

The U.S. postal service forwarded the envelope containing my Greencard to my address in Cape Town, though the legal specifications stipulate that the document only be sent to a U.S. address. Perhaps the employees of the post office in my northern American town broke the rules for someone they now recognised to be local enough.

On the day that I opened the envelope containing this laminated passcard, I drove back to the cottage on the de Trafford wine farm. At dusk, the light hits the westward faces of the mountains to a pink so unlikely that it seems as if the granite is transformed into roses. The stucco and brick Cape Dutch mansions in which the wine farm owners live impose on the landscapes around here: outsiders eager to signal their difference. Bits of my ancestors are all over – a Ceylonese woman is recorded as giving birth to the bastard child of Simon van der Stel, the Anglo-Indian first governor of the Cape. These leftovers are now the coloured workers on the farms, with generations of knowledge about how to trim the leaves around each bunch of grapes just right, so that the fruit will get the right amount of sun at harvest time: these are the new indentured servants of the Cape, whose ancestors hewed and laid down the stones for each of the grand homes lining the country roads.

I adored the language we in Southern Africa developed to explain our predicament: I knew how to speak of the gorgeous body of the pinotage in our glasses, the fat of the Karoo desert lamb in the roasting pan, and the way the granite on the mountain turned pink when the sun set – rather than face each other and speak cordially through our differences: this we had in common. To divert conflict, and the violence of the encounter that this landscape and these bodies had seen – and speak instead of the birdlife, the mountains, or of the body of one's lover – to map the territory of conquest with language sweet enough to distract: this was the fine art we had developed.

But the great and unmapped territory within, and the labour required for undertaking the cartography of the self – that courage we lacked.

I knew, then, that I was simply looking for a way out of aligning myself with the terrorist-ferreting, powerful nation at whose doorstep I did not want to beg – the nation that would solidify a powerful new identity for me the moment I flew back and faced the consequences of having paid a lawyer all my savings to engineer that mobility and belonging.

~

When I came back to my home university, located on the northern limit of my new country, I found an apartment with windows facing the shores of Lake Ontario – as close to the boundary of the nation as I could find. Above, beyond the lake and the horizon, were Canada and the Arctic Circle.

It was deep winter. In the evenings, locals park their cars on the bluffs facing the lake to watch winter waves leap up and over the breakwater wall, forming great frozen mounds with the energy and movement of each successive wave etched into the ice.

I woke up at 3am, the roar of the waves carried by the gusting arctic wind. Outside: blackness and water.

I could hear the burbling water-voices of the nightjars outside.

~

Author's Note on Miriam "Mazi" Makeba. From the dedication to *Chimurenga*, Volume 14. Makeba had 9 passports, and was given honorary citizenship in several countries; in 1960, she discovered that South Africa had revoked her passport when she tried to return for her mother's funeral; in '63, her citizenship was also revoked, after she testified against the apartheid system before the U.N. She, along with many others – including Nelson Mandela – didn't keep the "Passbook" that those classified as "Native" were required to carry. In South African slang, derived from Afrikaans, a "pass" can be a play on the word referring to a woman's sexuality: Miriam was known as a lover extraordinaire.

◊ ~◆~ ◊

"That to which we have been accustomed becomes, as it were,
a part of our nature."

- Aristotle

"Nothing human is foreign to me."

- motto of Earl Talbot

◊ ~◆~ ◊

An Immigrant's Deal:
Two Lives for the Price of One

Omer Hadžiselimović

When you become an immigrant, you have lost or are in the process of losing much: you lose your country, your language, your culture, your friends. But you also gain much: a new country, new knowledge, new experience, and perhaps new friends. The tension between the loss and the gain – or the debit and the credit side of your life's account – makes you feel as if you were living two lives, one you've left behind, and one you are living at the moment. You have not completely abandoned the old life, and you have not fully absorbed the new life.

When my family and I arrived in America, we changed not only continents but entire worlds, and that is always a difficult thing. It was difficult for me in spite of the fact that my professional life was deeply connected with our country of immigration: I was an English teacher at the University of Sarajevo, and my academic field was American Studies, the

147

study of the United States. In my classes in Sarajevo, I tried to explain something of American culture and history to myself and to my students – a hard task in both instances – but I liked the constant challenge of comparing American culture with my own. My approach was to incorporate material from history, literature, art, language, landscape studies, anthropology, and anything else that could capture and convey some telling essence of American life.

America has always struck me as so different from my part of the world that for a long time I thought of it as strange and exotic – from artifacts to sports to behavior patterns, from small things to big. This strangeness of America was, I'm sure, what attracted me to American Studies. I once compiled a catalog of the visibly different things a Southeastern European sees in the United States: windows that go up and down, like a guillotine, and do not open inside; doorknobs instead of handles; screens on doors and windows; water in toilet bowls; coiled rather than solid burners on the electric range; different measures and sizes; a different voltage; more static electricity; drinking fountains; relative absence of tobacco smoke; sports such as football and baseball; empty streets; lawns in front of homes (and lawn mowers, which provide a typical, inescapable American sound, as opposed to, for example, the equally inescapable European exact-time beep on the radio); heavily patterned wallpaper in contrast to lightly designed or blank wallpaper; wall calendars wrapped in cellophane and looking like old-fashioned LP albums; acronymic names of radio stations; shorter but wider printer paper.

Becoming an immigrant when you are an adult (say, middle-aged or older) is particularly hard because your previous life "interferes" with your immigrant life in more ways than you expected. So my two lives, the one in Bosnia (or former Yugoslavia), and the other here, in America, are constantly colliding, and I'm always comparing, contrasting my two lands, always "translating" from one into the other. This is of course true of my language situation, my linguistic identity, where translation of a kind always takes place between my native language and English. I "translate" between my two lives in other, perhaps less significant ways. Just to give you some examples, I still have to stop to think whether a date like, say, 08/06/06 is really August 6 or June 8 (as it would be in Europe), or whether Memorial Day or Labor Day falls in May (since in much of the rest of the world Labor Day is May 1), or how tall one is when measured in feet and inches, or what in centigrade is the temperature of 98F, often enriched with humidity, and whether it matches anything from my former experience (which it doesn't).

Common Boundary

As soon as you become an immigrant, everything irrevocably changes for you: space, landscape, the weather, the human geography – and even time. This last – time – turns against you: in the new country and in your new life, you are always behind; you want to catch up with things and events, to come up to the time level of everybody else because so much had happened when you weren't here. You badly need all kinds of practical information, for example, that you constantly ask questions, and that tends to make you feel outdated, lagging behind, and awkward. American society is more opaque in this fundamental informational sense: as a newcomer, you do not learn about people (individual people, their private lives, their power relationships) as easily as elsewhere. In America, in this sense, you feel that people generally do not know much about others, that the right hand does not know what the left hand is doing, as it were. But, strangely, this condition of ignorance in which you find yourself also makes you feel *younger,* like a young person asking basic questions, and gives you a sense of a new beginning, of learning, and exploring, of going through initiation. And starting from scratch keeps you on your toes.

By contrast, when you revisit the old country, in spite of the changes you see, your personal time seems to have stopped at the point of departure, since you remember a life there that is now permanently fixed in your memory. There, you are your old self (or you imagine you are) because you haven't lived through the changes that occurred. And that is how your old-country friends, acquaintances, and relatives see you – as your old self; what you do and how you live in the new country is of no real interest to them – there is hardly any curiosity about the new you. For all practical purposes, you have disappeared for them. You've truly "gone west" for them, as the old phrase has it: "gone west" was an American metaphor for dying. And you wonder if the people there have always been so self-referential or if they have become such only for you.

The immigrant is, psychologically, pulled back toward home by the power of memory, which is a major interference and something that insistently inhabits her/his new world. (Interference is also a linguistic term describing the obstacles presented by our native language when we try to learn a foreign language – it's always in the way, pulling us back, making it harder for us to master the strange new sounds and word order, for example.) This memory of the old things often starts with me as a visual representation, as images; so, for example, when I see Lake Michigan, close to which I now live, my subconscious thought is directed toward the Adriatic Sea, the large and familiar body of water in my former life and country; or when I see dark-blue clouds piling up on the horizon here, in the flat Midwest, they often appear to me, momentarily, as distant mountains, like those surrounding my hometown.   High-rise apartment buildings here, with tiny identical balconies suggesting congested living, buildings that I never appreciated as architecture, bring to mind the old country, the sense of sharing and of human closeness. And – perhaps most strangely – when I catch a whiff of cigarette smoke, a much rarer thing than in the old country, and I can't stand smoking, that immediately transports me to an earlier geography and to my earlier life.

All this is, of course, nostalgia, that constant companion of an immigrant's life. Although a universal human sentiment, nostalgia is hard to define precisely, and this is confirmed by interesting linguistic information: this concept is handled differently in different languages. The word "nostalgia," as Milan Kundera reminds us, comes from the Greek words "nostos" (return) and "algos" (suffering) – so, suffering because of the inability to return. But its different forms and nuances of meaning range widely in a number of European languages (and not all of them use the Greek-derived word primarily), describing a longing for home, a pain of absence, loneliness, or ignorance of what happens in the home country (Spanish *añoranza* [anjoransa], *añorar* – from Lat. *ignorare*).

Omer Hadžiselimović

Because of the distance traveled and the change experienced, home to the immigrant appears better and sweeter than it actually was, gaining a new, greater value. This feeling can occur when you actually return to the old country: When I am in my hometown of Sarajevo for short visits, the scent in the air on a summer night is uniquely intoxicating, like nothing I experience here in America, and those pine-wooded hills look more beautiful, now that I live elsewhere, than ever before. But nostalgia is mostly about missing people, those with whom I worked, lived, and shared a frame of reference. I miss the urban and urbane life of Sarajevo, its distinct sense of humor, its irony, both gentle and harsh, and its openness to the world. (But most of that was destroyed by the recent war anyway, so my nostalgia in this case is not merely geographic but "historical" – a longing for the past, which is another form of nostalgia. Bosnia, for me, is becoming a country of memory, to borrow Denis de Rougemont's description of Europe – "la patrie de la mémoire.")

Nostalgia, though a real feeling, is also a pleasant lie. "How handsome must our country be when seen and felt from outside!" writes the Spanish author Miguel de Unamuno. Another writer, the Nobel-Prize-winning V.S. Naipaul, offers in one of his novels, *A Bend in the River*, a practical cure for nostalgia – and that is frequent travel by plane:

> [T]he airplane is a wonderful thing. You are still
> in one place when you arrive at the other. The
> airplane is faster than the heart. You arrive quickly
> and you leave quickly. You don't grieve too much. . .
> . You can go back many times to the same place.
> You stop grieving for the past. You see that the past
> is something in your mind alone, that it doesn't exist
> in real life. You trample on the past, you crush it. In
> the beginning it is like trampling on a garden. In the
> end you are just walking on ground.

Absolute travel, it seems, destroys nostalgia absolutely. In this case, the duality of an immigrant's life truly becomes a reality, and perhaps not a painful one: the two lives can be lived almost simultaneously, not consecutively. But this cure for nostalgia – frequent travel by plane – tends to be expensive. Only the well-to-do can afford it. I know of a Sarajevan living in the United States, who often flies home for weekends, revisiting her mother and tasting Bosnian food. This certainly is a different experience of exile than, for example, what many Jews who fled from Spain after 1492 experienced in Bosnia, where for many generations they kept the keys to their houses with them, hoping to return; many families kept the key for generations, just as they clung to their religion, their Spanish language, and their songs.

There are other cures for nostalgia and hardships of immigrant life than frequent flights home – or throwing away your old house key. One is time, which cures everything, as we know, and the other is the immigrant's conscious effort to accept the new life as it comes, rationally and *positively*, as people in this country like to say – positive being a big word reflecting American cultural optimism, at least until the recent crises. Likewise, the immigrant's main dilemma – how to achieve a livable balance between the two lives, the balance between losing oneself to the new culture and standing apart from it – is often resolved in a natural way: by both retention and acceptance, retention of the old ways one wants or can keep, and acceptance of the new ways one wants or can accept. America, with its freedoms, has always been good at this, allowing so much leeway in people's private lives, and one can here think of religion, language, and other personal pursuits, or of cultivating such "un-American" activities like afternoon naps.

In my family, we have so far kept our language but of course use English with others and outside home, and we see no problem with it. We see no problem in starting a sentence in Bosnian and finishing it in English, or vice versa. Using two languages is certainly an advantage, not the least of which is that it exercises your brain. (It also enables you to gossip about other people in their presence.) Also, I use the two languages when I introduce myself and say my name, because

155

you have to use two sound systems when doing that – English and Bosnian/Croatian/Serbian. One can imagine what a challenge my last name presents to people with a short attention span. Paradoxically, my last name, which looks intimidating on paper, is only a paper tiger: it can be more easily pronounced in English than my first name, which is more complicated phonetically since it does not conform to English sounds.

Levity aside, the condition of immigration or exile makes you go through tough times (life puts you in your place – or America does), but it also offers you "certain rewards," "a double perspective" and fresh insights, as author Edward Said says; it offers you a place on the margin of the new culture, where you have an opportunity to see more than those in the center, that is, the inhabitants and original practitioners of that culture. That place on the margin gives you a certain freedom and possibilities of self-discovery, too. The Polish-American author Eva Hoffman, herself an immigrant, goes even further than Said when she notes that exile in modern times, and in postmodern theory, "becomes . . . sexy, glamorous, interesting," and that "nomadism and diasporism have become fashionable terms in intellectual discourse" because they connote "the virtues of instability, marginality, absence, and outsidedness." But Hoffman warns us that that sexiness and glamour of immigration come with much pain and loss.

So, like many recent immigrants who have come to this country as adults, I'm living my two lives, and I'm doing that both consecutively (I first lived there and now I'm living here) and simultaneously (although I now live here, I'm mentally living there, too). I'm living two lives for the price of one, and that, in commercial terms, is not a bad deal. But even in Bosnia I lived two lives, in a sense: one was my mundane, "real" life, and the other was my professional life, oriented toward America. I used to watch America from Bosnia; now I'm watching Bosnia from America, as I'm moving in my reading, research, and writing from American Studies to Balkan Studies. I used to be a Bosnian Americanist; here, I'm becoming an American Bosnianist. It's always more exciting to study that which is far away. But in another sense, my practical, teaching career has now come full circle, since I now do what I did before: I teach English to foreigners.

The longer I live in America, my two countries – or lives – are beginning to merge and converge; that is, my new country is beginning to look and feel more and more like my old country. Things and events here are beginning to assume *déjà vu* forms, as does my attitude towards them. I wonder if this is a psychological delusion or a process of true acclimatization. What, or who, has changed? I? My memory of the old country? The new country? All of the above? What seems to be true is that human nature and the nature of things show through the superficial differences: as time passes and as the newness and the romance of America fade, I see and experience here more of what reminds me of the old life. The two countries are becoming alike in a deep, universalizing sense – cause for both consolation and disappointment.

Exodus

Muriel Nelson

There are layers of customary gestures—

waves of handkerchiefs and hands
over sand, water, grassland, air,
of homesickness, of fevers, nausea, wounds, or worse, and if

there's more, then struggles back from speechlessness
>   *say how (can we sing) say*
>   *hello new money talk to them*
>   *say milk and honey people say bring shining*
>   *things to sun just imagine (pretend)*

when one foot sinks in mud or dust, the other itches
>   *fix it stitch up sky's hem clean strangeness decorate this*
>   *is how we immigrate how we start to nest and burn*
>   *letters from the rest send boxes say home dread*
>   *more cursives then dread none say home free in American.*

And some can only whisper after this,

some protect their daughters terribly,

some ride tractors off the earth,

some walk and carry on

~

The Widow Kramer

Ritzville, Washington, 1918

In billowing black, her pitchfork raised, she

chased a coyote out into her wheat.

Behind her: children,

horses, milk cow, chickens, geese,

ghost of a man,

sagebrush, mountain

range, width of a country, an ocean,

a sea, length of the Volga, a war,

ghost of the town

she called home.

Muriel Nelson

Emotional

To know, I thought, you have to feel your way
and aim your babysoft in the head toward birth.

Doctor, midwife, nurse, next you're newborn, and now
they wipe off all the bloody firmament.

The sun, that blind spot, tops your view. The violent
gases reign, blow, abrade, bellow. Shut

your eyes. You can tell it's still you, though you haven't taste
for dryness, the smell of it, the orphaning, the chill of nothing

holding you. You topple. Grasp. But
no flesh rescues. No word. Certainly,

no first person plural stretches long-armed
filaments with matching shadows' grand

crescendos. Reddish curtain. Close. It's not
the nineteenth century. Ready. Cut.

Uneasy Space

Your ground stretched out so far it took my height away,
so wide it held me in despair.

Wind groped there—nothing. Then the flat world tilted
to pour me back, and your game was over.

I had to move—for less, not more of that plain horizon—
where a wake of duck sliced sky from lake,
firs crimped its edges, gold stole the blue and wouldn't give it
                                                                    back,
then leaves laid it *down*, deep, layered; where

the high translucence of greens stood as an apricot tree
between sun and fall (and me)—*go* lights
with scarlet stems running sap after hot tips,
green-amber-red, almost all clear . . .

Muriel Nelson

from Pieces

If I could hold your face in both my hands
and you, so small in the distance, were my child
who did not hear,

you might use your eyes and seem to listen.
Then I'd use your eyes and sign to speak
as something ebbs and ebbs from them, minus

sound. But you're too far.
May you feel these waves, may they fill your eyes,
spill down your face, leave no more space between us.

◊ ~◆~ ◊

"Some minds improve by travel, others, rather,
Resemble copper wire or brass,
Which gets the narrower by going farther."

-    Thomas Hood

"Very weighty is the authority of custom."

-    Publilius Syrus

◊ ~◆~ ◊

Being a Foreigner

Azarin A. Sadegh

The day I left Iran for good in 1983, I had no idea what living as a foreigner really meant.

Now I do.

Being a foreigner – no matter where I am – I always comprehend at most half of what people say.

It means not getting the punch line of the story, not making connections between an old TV show character and something that is happening at the moment. I feel as if I've been thrown onstage to play a role I haven't learned yet. I feel as if I'm trapped at night in a labyrinth, trying to find the exit.

Being a foreigner means I've lost the deep sense of belonging to a place. It feels like an endless struggle just to try to look like everybody else, just to have a banal discussion at work, to offer a neighbor details of a soup recipe, to tell my child a night-time story. It means never being completely in the present, like being half deaf, or half blind, or half retarded. Almost half alive, half dead. It means having to say, "What did you mean?" 100 times a day.

Common Boundary

Being a foreigner means that even if I go back to my own country, I will still be a foreigner because I would not feel the same worries as those living in Iran today. I would not laugh at their jokes. I would not cry at their endless funerals. I would not pray to their unashamed god. I would not follow their rules. I would not listen to their noise, their silence. I would not lie to pretend to be something that I am not. I would not look like them. And still, I would have to answer this question: "Where do you come from?" 100 times a day.

Being a foreigner means I can't really understand my own children's words. It means I am a mother who is never going to be there, fully, for them, never sharing their deepest feelings, their deepest fears, never able to heal their wounds.

Living as a foreigner is like playing a guessing game. Most of us lose this game. Some of us, after years of trying, finally succeed in dragging ourselves to the top where ordinary life quietly flows.

I thought I was there, at the top.

Until one day I heard that the USA might start a war with Iran.

~

I really don't know what I am supposed to feel. What am I allowed to say? Am I living in a free country as I always thought I was?

Azarin A. Sadegh

I left Iran without any regrets. And still I think of my leaving as an accomplishment. Still I think I am living right now in "heaven on earth."

But why don't I feel happy? Why doesn't this place feel like the promised land? The prospect of a war with Iran has broken the illusion of happiness. It is burning my heaven.

What if I am not really happy?

I am not sure what I will feel if U.S. bombs destroy my childhood house, the house that I hated, if those bombs kill my childhood friends who weren't really my friends, if they hurt my aunts, my cousins, my nephews whose names I have never learned.

And I am just so tired of the mountain of hatred in my nightmares.

~

Being a foreigner means accepting hatred. It means forgetting whatever is left from this vast distance in time connecting me to the past, a place I have no right to own, to remember, to love. Because I left. In the act of leaving those memories, I have sworn not to remember them, ever.

What if the U.S. bombs, like a faraway smell, like a sweet taste, like a familiar image, bring back those anguished, lonely moments I have escaped?

Common Boundary

What if with the sound of each explosion, I wake up at the bottom, where I have always remained.

~

Being a foreigner means speaking without being understood.

Blue Painted Field

Tim Nees

Sennick glances around the room but nothing seems clear. It is hard for him to make out the shape of the place, his orientation within it, impossible for him to understand why he is there. The harder he searches for something to latch on to, the less he sees. Walls dissolve in sky-blue cloud, tease his sense of balance. Everything in the room floats in blue. He thinks he sees a window and a table but, from where he stands, they could be one and the same.

In all other respects the room appears ordinary and anonymous, mainly due to an apparent emptiness, although he cannot tell if anything remains concealed. He hopes it will prove to be completely ordinary, given that surprises can be difficult and he's had his fair share of those over the years, but he admits that's unlikely to be the case. Not under his present circumstances. So he describes the room as plain, much like any other room in any building in any street in any city in any country in the world, except for the possibility of it having five corners instead of four, which puts him on the back foot once more. He counts them but loses his place, the margins fugitive. The room gives the uncanny impression that it is a part of his childhood home, a home half-remembered, a room he may have been taken to and left for disciplinary purposes, a room he would never venture into on his own.

He stands close to where the door had been but is no longer, less than halfway to a table he sees more clearly now, in the middle but not the centre of the room. The window is mounted high, an empty picture-frame on the wall, well above dado height, except there is no dado. The wall rises smoothly then slips effortlessly into the void of the ceiling. Sennick scratches the stubble on his chin measuring its growth while, at the same time, trying better to determine the dimensions of the space surrounding him. He's not at all certain if there are side walls or end walls, or in which wall the window sits. It could just as well be an opening in the ceiling and the ceiling could just as well be the floor.

Shapes that could be chair, hat-rack, bookcase, lamp, pulse dimly in the room, neither foreground nor background, unsure of their role as furnishings. They too appear blue but their blueness is less innate, as if they've been hastily camouflaged. A skin of paint, an accumulation of dust or ash, each surface laden and sinking in the oppressive atmosphere. The only contrast is in the blue-grey folds of his jacket hanging limply from a hook, the shadows resembling the features of a mask discarded, now ritual has ended.

Sennick shuffles forward and touches his jacket but is not reassured. He can't recall hanging it there. Perhaps he'd come here earlier in the day. But which day is today, anyway? Time has passed – or has it? – since his so-called "interruption." It is definitely daytime, judging from the hazy light penetrating the room, unless he's been tricked and a sodium sun burns falsely outside that tiny window. Is there any way of knowing? There is no watch strapped to his pastel wrist. He trembles and thrusts his hands into the pockets of his gown to stop from shaking.

His blue slippers scrape the floor. He stops. He starts. He stops again. The sound of scuffling fills the room. He sighs, catches his breath, then, in a slow steady stream, exhales. The feeble noise sounds loud in the dense air, as if a contact microphone's been stuck to his lips.

He rubs his chin and recalls his reflection in the mirror in the other room, the room that must have been for bathing, his grey hair heavy with cheap oil and spattered with bluish flecks as his shadowed face stared back at him, looking older than he imagined he should. He feels even older now. He wishes he'd had the chance to wash. His shoulders slump. He sags, defeated by the sound of his own breathing.

Common Boundary

Sennick remembers several pairs of hands touching him in the washroom. Black hands or blue, blue faded to a transparent shade that was barely blue at all, or black, some a dense black, so black they were blue. One aspect of their fingers struck him as unusual. Had they been wearing gloves, black gloves, had their hands been covered with powder, blue powder, or talc? He had barely felt their touch. Did blue hands really pull him from that room, dress him in this shabby gown, demean him? They may have done so, or he may have propelled himself. He cannot recall how it went, any passages or doors, whether he was carried or made to crawl, who led and who followed. Being there and being here remain discrete events rendered ambiguous through dislocation.

The window seems closer than before but it's hard to tell, blue sky in a blue wall. He saw a painting like this once, the only difference was the brushstrokes clearly visible, which gave it away as a painting and not captured sky. Titled *Blue Painted Field,* which seemed odd as it was obviously sky, though the attendant mumbled something that sounded like "cornflowers," but she spoke in the wrong language and no-one could translate.

Sennick tries to walk to the window, better to see the day outside. He takes a step down one side of the table, then three more, one after the other, but falters halfway. The room tips. He grips the edge of the table and shuffles sideways, hand over hand, seeking the chair he hopes is somewhere near. He pauses at the corner, the corner which should have been opposite the lamp, then creeps back around the table watched by the hat-rack and the window pane.

The sun momentarily returns bleaching the walls from blue to pastel, making his journey even more hazardous, until the clouds blanket it once more. Five minutes pass before he completes the circuit and grabs the chair, sitting heavily with a sob. The empty bookcase abrades him, the hat-rack prickly, the lamp dark. His old world distant, yet its weight can be felt pressing against the absent door, the walls, against poor Sennick, uncertain of his place this side of nowhere, and how he should behave with no rules.

His hands cup his head, elbows resting on the table. He pulls his splayed feet together and shudders as the whisk of his slippers echoes in the room, pushes his stubby fingers through his lank hair and inspects two strands fallen in front of him, their greyness blued as if he's been given a gentian rinse, tries to blow the hairs across the table but they stick stubbornly in place, crosses both arms over his chest as if he's cold or shielding himself from an indistinct threat, drops hands to lap, circles thumbs, clasps fingers, stares intently at the plateau of the plain blue table. A blue man in a sky blue room, lost, present, mute; resident or foreign, depends on the point of view. His eyelids flutter. Relieved from the weight so demanding on his legs, but not which afflicts his mind.

Four objects materialise on the table, each of them blue, formed from matter drawn from the five corners of the room. Sennick watches as each shape becomes a thing, things he recognises or thinks he should: a bird, a hat, a book, a lake.

The bird is flightless. Vestiges of what may once have been wings are so malformed they serve no useful purpose, even if the bird possessed the musculature to move them. The bird's beauty, then, lies in its feathers, so small and fine and such a rich blue. His grandmother called the colour jajaya – or was it jaiya? – he's forgotten the correct pronunciation. The colour-word became the naming-word for the bird, he remembers that much. But it may have been no more than a childish word his grandmother invented to lull him to sleep. The highly prized feathers, however, were woven into cloaks to adorn the women on the day of their betrothal. He'd found that story depressing when his grandmother told him one day.

On the table the bird does not move. Extinct since before Sennick was born, his only exposure through stories and the remains of cloaks displayed in cases in the state museum. But it stares back at him, this bird, through faintly accusing eyes. Where have you been, it asks. Why have you forgotten so much? The beak long and slightly curved, the bird has only to nod slightly and it will strike the table top, producing a resonant beat similar to a wooden drum struck with a stick. Sennick taps his fingers on the table but he's out of time and the noise deafens. He stops.

His past is full of the tintinnabulations of rainfall on thin tin roofs, the rattle of the balafon, hands slapping calabashes in celebration, though both instruments had been imported from other lands. He hears their music now but it soon muddles, a truck rumbling down a gravel road.

The hat resembles one he could have picked up off the pavement outside one of the many music clubs that had been in his neighbourhood. Perhaps he'd found one similar, one night so late morning delivery vans already buzzed the streets, and as he left the club, music ringing in his ears, he watched it roll his way, oddly like a weighted ball. He grabbed it before it hit the gutter. The hat is familiar. His uncle had a hat like this, the same in all respects except the colour. He wore it when he sang. His had been cream and the band olive green. A badge pinned to the front near the crown. A silver badge with a coat of arms, the jaiya bird standing on a gourd, talons gripping tight as tree roots. But the hat on the table hasn't a badge, not even a blue one. The loss of detail upsets Sennick.

He wishes he'd noticed it earlier. He'd like to take a feather and insert it in the band. He'd like to remember a song.

Next to the bird a book lies open. Thin with deckled edges, its pages rise from the centre in a double curve like wings the bird should have had but hasn't. Type falls to the margins and rises back again, the paper almost translucent, blue like cold skin, old skin, veins dimly visible. The alphabet is familiar though marks have been added above or below, marks he's not seen before, accents helping the reader to keep in rhythm, to stress certain syllables, alter sounds within words, such instructions fixed by custom. It sounds plausible but he doesn't know for sure. It could be musical notation.

He turns his attention to two illustrations, one in each corner of the page. A manta ray swims left, blue and eerily magnificent. Its wings caress the water in a way that appears as if the image is actually moving, as in a film clip. In the background a headland, everything rendered blue. The scene is the strait leading into the harbour, captured on a winter's day. How long it's been since he's seen a ray in that harbour.

The other image shows the dark centre of a forest, tree trunks clustered, their roots break the ground, the leaf canopy out of frame but heavily present, blocking light from above. A thick blue gloom, not unlike the air in the room, hangs between the trunks. Nothing moves. Is this what has happened to the woods he used to play in as a child?

There is a lake up a winding path through the trees. The lake is on the table. A small lake shaped like a jigsaw piece. Flat and still, it could have been cut from a sheet of glass or mirror. The real lake had herons and reeds, fine ferns thick along the shore. A lake formed in myth when a girl's tears flowed from a mountain where her lover, caught in a blizzard, lost his life. The lake has a name, but he's misplaced it, and he hasn't the energy to invent a new one. It was probably the name of the girl. It might be written in the book.

He wonders what these things signify and who put them here, if they're present at all. If the table, though solid beneath his elbows, is just a prop and all it will take is some gesture, some word, for everything to dissolve in mist then reform and taunt him as memories do, only to twist and turn and vanish altogether. His slippers scrape the floor as he stands, hesitating at the table edge, afraid to touch what once was only too real for him and his family. But where are they? He searches for the door, but there is only the window, a painted square of cloudy blue.

It's too soon to panic, to jump to assumptions, to play the games others want him to play. He could leave at any time. It wouldn't take much to create a gap. Find a corner and push against both walls until they part like flimsy pages. He wants to turn another page, inspect the plates that might be there, unravel the meaning of the awkward script.

He reaches for the book surrounded by water, the hat beside the bird perched on the book at the end of the table, but his arms are heavy and stiff. The backs of his hands repulse him, thin wrists and pale mottled skin. He pulls them out of sight. He wishes he had a cigarette. Perhaps the thick air will suffice. But so much blue is making him nauseous. Unsurprisingly he weeps and cannot stop. Water washes his slippers. Cold penetrates his skin. He has never felt as acutely unfamiliar in his life as he feels at this moment.

Biographical Notes on Contributors –
Including Previous Publication Acknowledgments

Janice Eidus lives in Brooklyn, New York and San Miguel de Allende, Mexico. "The Color of Cinnamon" was previously published in *Dirt: The Quirks, Habits, and Passions of Keeping House*, edited by Mindy Lewis (Seal Press, 2009). She's won two O. Henry Prizes. Her novels include *The War of the Rosens* and *Urban Bliss*; her story collections are *Vito Loves Geraldine* and *The Celibacy Club*. She is co-editor of *It's Only Rock and Roll: An Anthology of Rock and Roll Short Stories*. Her forthcoming novel is *The Last Jewish Virgin*.

Omer Hadžiselimović, formerly Professor of English at the University of Sarajevo, Bosnia, is now Adjunct Professor of English at Loyola University Chicago. He has authored two books and several dozen articles, reviews, and translations in American Studies, English literature, Bosnian literature, and travel writing. His book *At the Gates of the East* on English travelers in Bosnia appeared in 2001.

John Guzlowski's writing appears in *The Ontario Review, Exquisite Corpse*, and other journals. His poems about his parents' experiences in Nazi concentration camps appear in his book *Lightning and Ashes*. Regarding the Polish edition of these poems, Nobel Laureate Czeslaw Milosz says the poems are "astonishing." Guzlowski blogs about his parents' experiences: lightning-and-ashes.blogspot.com

Roy Jacobstein is the author of five collections of poetry, including *Fuchsia in Cambodia* (Northwestern U Press, 2008), *A Form of Optimism* (UPNE, 2006, Morse Prize), and *Ripe* (U Wisconsin Press, 2002, Pollak Prize). His work has received the James Wright Poetry Prize and the American Anthropology Association's Humanistic Poetry Prize, and is included in *LITERATURE: Reading Fiction, Poetry & Drama* (Mc-Graw-Hill, 2006). "Ceremony" appears in *Fuchsia in Cambodia* and "Emigrées" in *A Form of Optimism*. Both "Passover" and "Beyond the Gauze Curtain" appear in *Ripe*.

M. Neelika Jayawardane is Assistant Professor of English and Director of Interdisciplinary Studies at SUNY-Oswego. She was born in Sri Lanka, and grew up in a mining town in Copperbelt

Province, Zambia. She received her Master's and Bachelor's degrees from Iowa State University, and a doctorate from the University of Denver. She has been a Visiting Associate at the University of Cape Town since 2005. A longer version of "Pass" appeared as follows: M. Neelika Jayawardane, "Life in Transit/Love is a Homesickness," http://reconfigurations.blogspot.com/2009/11/m-neelika-jayawardane-life-in-transit.html, RECONFIGURATIONS: A Journal for Poetics & Poetry/ Literature & Culture, v. 3: Immanence / Imminence, ed. W. Scott Howard (November, 2009).

Rivka Keren (born as Katalin Friedländer in Debrecen, Hungary, July 24, 1946) is an Israeli writer. She immigrated to Israel in 1957 and studied painting, philosophy, literature and clinical psychology. So far, she has published fourteen books for adults, adolescents and children, won numerous literary prizes and has been translated into English, German, Spanish, Russian, Hungarian and Braille. Her novels and stories are a study of human nature, the destructiveness of evil and revenge, and the power of hope and love. Rivka Keren is married with two children. For further details go to en.wikipedia.org/wiki/Rivka_Keren

Eva Konstantopoulos was born in New York City and raised in nearby Rockland County, N.Y. Her short stories have previously appeared in *The Salt River Review, Storyglossia,* and *SLAB,* among others. Currently, she lives and writes in Los Angeles.

Dagmara J. Kurcz was born and raised in Wroclaw, Poland. At the age of twelve, she came to Chicago, where she settled in a predominantly Polish neighborhood. She received her MA in Teaching of Writing from Columbia College, Chicago. She lives in Northlake, Illinois, with her husband Krzysztof, and daughter Kaya. She teaches at Triton Community College.

Mitch Levenberg has published essays and short fiction in such journals as *The Common Review, Fiction, The New Delta Review, The Saint Ann's Review, Confluence,* and others. His collection of stories, *Principles of Uncertainty and Other Constants* was published in March 2006. He teaches writing and Literature at St. Francis College and at New

York University and lives in Brooklyn with his wife, daughter and four dogs.

Cassandra Lewis is the writer at Bastille Arts. Her plays have been performed in London, New York, Chicago, and San Francisco. *Migrations* was a finalist in the New by Northwest Competition. Notable publishing credits include: *The Best Plays of The Strawberry One-Act Festival Anthology* and *Mother/Daughter Monologues: Babes and Beginnings*. She is a member of The Dramatists Guild and PEN USA.

Tim Nees is a writer living in Wellington, New Zealand. He has been published recently in literary journals *JAAM* 27 2009, *NZ Poetry* 38 2009 and 40 2010, and the anthology *Pain and Memory*, (Editions Bibliotekos 2009). Tim was runner up in NZ Post Wellington Sonnet Competition 2008, and on the Premier Shortlist for BNZ Katherine Mansfield Short Story Competition 2009. He was recently nominated for a Pushcart Prize.

Muriel Nelson has two collections of poems, *Part Song* (Bear Star Press, 1999) and *Most Wanted* (ByLine Press, 2003). Nominated twice for the Pushcart Prize, her work has appeared in *The New Republic, Ploughshares, Beloit Poetry Journal, The Massachusetts Review,* and others. She teaches at Pierce College in Washington State. Previous publication acknowledgments: "The Widow Kramer," *Part Song* (Bear Star, 1999) and *Washington English Journal* 22.2 (2000): 7; "Emotional," *Most Wanted* (ByLine, 2003); "*from* Pieces" *Part Song* (Bear Star, 1999); "Uneasy Space," *Drought: A Literary Review.* 10 Feb. 2001.

George Rabasa is the author of a short-story collection and three novels, most recently *The Wonder Singer* in 2008. A new novel, *Ms Entropia and the Adam Bomb*, is forthcoming from Unbridled Books. He was born in Maine and lived many years in Mexico City, until the search for the ideal climate took him to Minnesota. "The Unmasking of El Santo" was previously published by the Walker Art Center, Minneapolis in an exhibition catalogue.

Nahid Rachlin's publications include a memoir, *Persian Girls* (Penguin), four novels, *Jumping Over Fire* (City Lights), *Foreigner*

(W.W. Norton), *Married to a Stranger* (E.P. Dutton), *The Heart's Desire* (City Lights), and a collection of short stories, *Veils* (City Lights). Her short stories have been published in about fifty magazines. As a student she held a Doubleday-Columbia fellowship and a Wallace Stegner Fellowship (Stanford). The grants and awards she has received include, the Bennet Cerf Award, PEN Syndicated Fiction Project Award, and a National Endowment for the Arts grant. Her website: www.nahidrachlin.com

Ruth Sabath Rosenthal is a New York poet, published in numerous literary journals and poetry anthologies in the U.S. and internationally. Journals: *Connecticut Review; Birmingham Review; Ibbetson Stree; Mobius-The Poetry Magazine; Pacific Review; Sarasvati; Taj Mahal Review; Vallium*. Anthologies: *Harvest of New Millennium; Songs of Seasoned Women; Pain & Memory; The Book of Ten; Voices Israel*. Ruth's poem "on yet another birthday," was nominated for a Pushcart Prize by *Ibbetson Street*. "Into the Light" has previously been published: *Poetica; MungBeing Magazine; Empty Shoes* (Popcorn Press, 2009), ed. Patrick T. Randolph; primal sanities! *a Tribute to Walt Whitman* (Allbook Books, 2008), eds. Mankh (Walter E. Harris III) and George Wallace; *Mizmor L'David Anthology: Volume I – Holocaust* (Poetica Press, 2010), ed. Michal Mahgerefteh; *Voices Israel 2008*. www.ruthsabathrosenthal.moonfruit.com

Azarin A. Sadegh is an Iranian-American writer and poet, living in Los Angeles. "Being a Foreigner" was first published in Chicago Sun Times. Other work has been published in Ashena and Iranian.com. She has also participated in a cyber-anthology, *The Other Voice Project*, listed in the journal section of the World Poetry Directory of UNESCO. She is currently working on her second novel.

Ruth Knafo Setton is the author of the critically acclaimed novel, *The Road to Fez*. Born in Safi, Morocco, she is the recipient of literary fellowships from the National Endowment of the Arts, Pennsylvania Council on the Arts and PEN. Her poetry, fiction and creative nonfiction have appeared in many journals and anthologies. The Writer-in-Residence for the Berman Center for Jewish Studies at Lehigh University, she is working on a new novel and a poetry collection. Two short paragraphs of "Living Between Question

Marks," were previously published in Ruth's novel, *The Road to Fez* (Counterpoint Press, 2001), and from an interview that was published in *The Forward* (21 January 2005) entitled, "Sephardic Arts and Culture: A Dialogue." "My Father Eats Figs" was previously published in the online journal, *InPosse Review* (Summer, 2001).

Patty Somlo has been nominated for the Pushcart Prize and was a finalist in the Tom Howard Short Story Contest. Her stories have appeared in *The Santa Clara Review, The Sand Hill Review, Under the Sun, Switchback, Fringe Magazine,* and in the anthologies, *Voices From the Couch* and *Bombshells: War Stories and Poetry by Women on the Homefront.* "How He Made it Across" was previously published in the Spring 2009 issue of *The November 3rd Club.*

Rewa Zeinati is a poet, translator, writer, editor, and painter. Her poems and translations have been published in journals such as *Natural Bridge Journal, Mizna, Al Jadid Journal, Santa Clara Review, Lamplighter Review,* The English PEN Online World Atlas, as well as Poets Against War. She's just moved back to the Middle East after living in the U.S. for seven years and continues to write, paint, doodle and celebrate renewal.

≈≈≈◆≈≈≈

◊ ~◆~ ◊

ABOUT EDITIONS BIBLIOTEKOS

Mission and Goals: To produce books of literary merit that address important issues, complex ideas, and enduring themes. To publish in book form contemporary voices that might not otherwise be heard; each author's work will appear in print among good company. That's the best we can do, but we think it is enough.

For a petit publisher, creating original collections is a time-consuming and tedious process, but well worth the effort in producing texts worth reading and studying for years to come. Was it in our destiny to become publishers? We are students of philosophy, literature, and history; we are scholars, academics, and writers – humanists. We are not business people, but somewhere in our intellectual journey we felt more acutely than usual the joy and pain associated with writing and publishing and then made the decision to shepherd other people's work (their voices) into print.

If you like this book, read (also by Bibliotekos), *Pain and Memory: Reflections on the Strength of the Human Spirit in Suffering* (2009).

www.ebibliotekos.blogspot.com